The Caper

Nancy Rue

BETHANY HOUSE PUBLISHERS
MINNEAPOLIS, MINNESOTA 55438

Published by Bethany House Publishers
A Ministry of Bethany Fellowship International
11400 Hampshire Avenue South
Minneapolis, Minnesota 55438
www.bethanyhouse.com

Printed in the United States of America by
Bethany Press International, Minneapolis, Minnesota 55438

Library of Congress Cataloging-in-Publication Data

Rue, Nancy N.
    The caper / Nancy Rue.
        p. cm. — (Christian heritage series. The Chicago years; 5)
    Summary: While staying with his elderly aunt on Cape Cod for the summer and trying to
follow his father's charge to keep himself and his sister and brother out of trouble, Rudy is
worried about his flamboyant uncle's professed conversion by a charismatic preacher and the
mysterious, possibly dangerous, dealings of some shadowy characters he meets on the beach.
    ISBN 1-56179-837-1
    [1. Brothers and sisters—Fiction. 2. Christian life—Fiction. 3. Evangelists—Fiction.
4. Criminals—Fiction. 5. Cape Cod (Mass.)—Fiction.] I. Title.
PZ7.R88515 Cak 2000
[Fic]—dc21   99-056189
                                                                              CIP

01   02   03   04   /   10   9   8   7   6   5   4   3   2   1

For Granny Verna Nollner,
A delightful child of the Twenties

Chapter One

O n the counta three, Rudolpho!" Little Al called out from his spot on top of the sand dune.

"Ready!"

"And don't forget—you have to run over at least one clump of grass and not fall down!" That came from Hildy Helen, Rudy Hutchinson's twin sister, who was also at the top of the sand dune, still straddling her bike and breathing hard from *her* successful run downhill. "So far the record's three!"

"I *know*!" Rudy said between his teeth. He hoped she wouldn't add that *she* was the one who currently held that record. If she did, he'd have to give her a sand shower. Rudy straightened his knickers and tried to concentrate.

"Coast is clear!" Little Al shouted. "One . . . two . . . thr—"

Rudy flipped the glob of curls off the top of his wire-rimmed glasses and pushed down hard on the pedals. Riding in sand was like running in a bad dream—you never could get anywhere. But it was worth a try to beat out the two of them. They won at *everything* these days, now that Rudy wasn't—

But there was no time to finish the thought. Coming up, there

1

was a huge clump of silvery green grass that sprouted up who knew how in the sand, and he had to be ready for it. You lost points for every time you flubbed the dub.

Rudy steered straight for it, biting his lower lip in concentration. Above him, he could vaguely hear Little Al shouting something.

"Don't bother me!" Rudy yelled back, and he hit the grass clump head on. *Hang onto the handlebars,* he could imagine Hildy Helen reminding him for the hundredth time. Although he did, he wasn't prepared for the way they jerked. The bicycle slid sideways, and Rudy started to go with it, glasses askew. Now he *could* hear Hildy Helen shouting to him, probably a whole paragraph's worth of instructions, and Rudy bit down harder on his lip and swerved the bike back on track.

Grinning triumphantly, he glanced up over his shoulder. "I didn't go down!" he yelled.

He straightened his glasses and whipped his face forward again to look for another clump, but the image he'd just seen on top of the dune stayed in his head like a silent movie: Little Al and Hildy Helen waving their arms and pointing as if the Mob were after them.

If they'd been in Chicago, Rudy would have ditched the bike and dived for the nearest hole. But this was Cape Cod—

There was no time to finish *that* thought, either. For just as Rudy wobbled his way around the last hill of sand and headed for the road, he saw out of the corner of his eye exactly what his brother and sister were doing a dune dance about.

There was a car coming, and not just any car. It was Aunt Gussie's long, pink 1929 Pierce Arrow.

Rudy jammed back on the pedals to stop the bike. He could tell that Sol, Aunt Gussie's driver, was standing on his brakes, too, for the tires sprayed white fragments from the packed-down-clamshell road, and the rear end slid sideways like the tail of a marlin. But it wasn't stopping fast enough, and neither was the bike.

Rudy jerked the handlebars hard to the right until he thought he'd pull his arm completely out of its socket. The bike hit another clump of silver-green grass and this time did a fishtail in mid-air. It came down with a crunch on the side of the road, and Rudy could feel the heat coming out the side of the Pierce Arrow just inches from his head.

He rolled over in time to see one of the pink doors come open and his father leap out, already running his hand through his wavy, dark hair. Rudy groaned, but not from the plaster of shells on the side of his face. It was more in anticipation of the look his father was going to have in his eyes. Rudy felt for his glasses and stuck them back on.

"Rudy, for the love of Mike!" Dad said. "Are you all right?"

Rudy pushed the bike off himself and spit out some yellow-brown grit. Little Al was already there beside him, sticking out a hand to pull him up.

"You know how he is, Mr. Hutchie," Al said. "Athletic stuff's not exactly his cuppa tea, if you know what I mean."

"Athletic? This isn't athletic, it's crazy! What were you three doing?"

"Headin' you off at the pass," Little Al said.

"You've been listening to entirely too much radio." That came from LaDonna as she approached with her flowing walk from the car. She was a Hutchinson, too, even though she was a Negro, and was Aunt Gussie's maid Quintonia's niece, and now Dad's secretary in his law office for the summer. It was hard enough for Rudy to keep straight when he wasn't busy emptying his mouth of Cape Cod beach.

"You were doing what?" Dad said.

"We were just having a contest," Hildy Helen said as she joined them. She tossed her short, bobbed hair proudly. "I was winning."

"A contest to see who could kill himself first?" Dad said. Rudy watched his eyes closely. They were stern behind his gold-rimmed, round glasses, but they didn't have the look Rudy dreaded—not yet, anyway.

"We didn't even see you coming," Hildy Helen said.

"Sure you didn't," Rudy mumbled.

Hildy Helen wrinkled her nose at him. "Where are you going, anyway?" she said to Dad.

"Back to Chicago," Dad said. "Sol's driving us to the train station in Eastham."

Rudy stopped spitting sand. "Now?" he said. "I thought you weren't going until tomorrow."

"I just got word that I have a new case," Dad said. "I thought we ought to get back and get right on it."

Three faces fell. Not LaDonna's. She remained calm as she picked a few bits of clam shell off her yellow chemise. She was only 17, but sometimes she was as no-nonsense as Aunt Gussie herself.

"Then it's a good thing we were here," Hildy Helen said. Then she stuck her bottom lip out. "At least we get to say good-bye."

"You could have gotten yourselves maimed in the process," Dad said. "I think you three could stir up trouble anywhere, even out here on the Outer Cape. I never saw a group of 11-year-olds who could find it the way you do."

"Thanks, Mr. Hutchie!" Little Al puffed out his chest the way he did when he was particularly pleased with himself. His dark eyes were sparkling.

"I didn't mean it as a compliment," Dad said. "I don't want trouble this summer. I want you to have a quiet, normal childhood experience." He began rolling up one sleeve of his striped shirt, and Hildy Helen started in on the other one for him.

"It's fun being on the ocean and everything," she said, "but, Dad, it's really kind of boring here. Can't I go back to Chicago with you and LaDonna? I could help in the office, too—"

"No, thank you!" LaDonna said, and she straightened her yellow cloche hat for punctuation.

"We've had this conversation before," Dad said. "And if we have it again, it's going to be exactly the same." His voice had an edge of weariness. Rudy hoped that meant they *wouldn't* have the discussion again. But Hildy Helen, of course, couldn't leave it alone.

"You said yourself things were changing in Chicago, and you've made some of those changes happen yourself, right?"

"She's got a point, Mr. Hutchie," Little Al said. "And with Al Capone in jail, what's to worry about?"

Dad looked at Little Al. "Now that's a joke, and you know it. He's in jail in Philadelphia, yes, but he put himself there—went willingly—because he knew he was about to be killed by rival gangs in New York, if not Chicago itself. He had his arrest arranged, for Pete's sake, and I hear tell he has a desk in his cell, unlimited visitors, use of the warden's phone." He narrowed his eyes. "As long as he can contact his people, he's just as dangerous behind bars as he is on the outside. We can't underestimate a man who has probably had 200 people killed and has never been convicted. Besides, it isn't just about the Mob."

Hildy Helen sighed like a movie star. *Greta Garbo*, Rudy thought, *would have been proud*.

"We know, Dad," she said, rolling her brown eyes. "You and Aunt Gussie want us out here in nature, away from all those people who don't believe in the right things anymore."

She sighed dramatically yet again, but it was lost on Dad. He looked up over the sand dunes with that fuzzy look he always got when he was thinking serious thoughts.

"Nothing is sacred anymore," he said. "Ever since the war, there are no traditions, no cherished beliefs. We've got people telling us we are the direct descendants of monkeys. That keeping ourselves from doing whatever we jolly well please is going to turn us all into lunatics. That some baseball player deserves more respect than our founding fathers."

"Now you gotta admit, Mr. Hutchie," Little Al said, "that Babe Ruth is a little more interesting than George Washington."

"That's what bothers me—the things that interest people these days." Dad went on about how people gobbled up scandals in the newspapers like a bunch of bottom feeders.

Hildy Helen studied the ends of her hair.

Little Al buried his left foot in the sand.

Rudy propped his eyes open and nodded at his father and tried not to look half asleep.

It wasn't that Rudy didn't believe Dad. He figured he understood what Dad was talking about more than Hildy Helen and Little Al did. And he had definitely learned enough since he'd lived in Chicago to know you had to be responsible about this stuff.

But being responsible, and hearing about being responsible over and over, sure could be dull.

"Am I making any sense at all?" Dad said.

"Yes!" Rudy said before Hildy Helen could jump in and drag this out even longer.

She still couldn't resist one more stab at it. "I know it's safe and peaceful and good and all that, but what about excitement?"

Dad gave her a hard stare, and Rudy cringed. Dad's eyes lost their fuzzy look. "You three have had enough excitement for a while," he said.

"So you're really going to leave us here for two months." Hildy Helen's lip came out again.

"Yes."

"And you're not even coming back for a visit until—"

"Hildy Helen, dummy *up*!" Rudy said.

She tossed her bob, but she got quiet.

"Mr. Jim, if we're going to catch that train . . ." LaDonna looked firmly at the car, and Sol slipped back into it and started the motor.

Dad reached out both arms and pulled Hildy Helen into one and Little Al into another.

"Behave," he said, "or there will be consequences, do you hear?"

"Yes, sir, Mr. Hutchie. You got my word," Little Al said.

That seemed good enough for Dad. After all, Little Al knew that if he got into any serious trouble, the judge was going to take him away from Aunt Gussie and Dad and send him to jail.

But Dad gave Hildy Helen a hard look, and she gave the Greta Garbo sigh again. "I sure liked it better when you were so wrapped up in your work, you didn't know *what* we were doing," she said.

"You don't mean that," Dad said and gave her a squeeze. Over her head, he looked at Rudy and nodded toward the dune. "I'd like a word with you in private before I go, son," he said.

Rudy's heart suddenly felt like a boulder. It was even harder to follow Dad through the sand on foot than it was to steer his bike through it, his feet were so heavy with I-don't-want-to-do-this. To make it worse, when they reached a spot that Dad seemed to feel was far enough away from Little Al and Hildy Helen's hearing, the look Rudy had been dreading was firm in Dad's eyes. It was the look that said, *Rudy, I'm disappointed in you.* Rudy's heart fell all the way to his knees.

"Sorry about the sand dune race, Dad," Rudy said hurriedly. "They didn't tell me anybody was coming and—"

"Rudy." Dad put a hard hand on Rudy's shoulder that stopped everything—his speech, his heart, the world. "It's just that I have come to expect more of you. I'm depending on you to make sure that there is no foolishness while I'm away. It's up to *you*, son. Not Aunt Gussie. You know she hasn't been the same since her stroke. Dr. Kennedy says she cannot be upset in any way or it's liable to happen again, and she might not bounce back this time. She isn't a young woman—"

Please stop, Rudy thought miserably. *I already feel like chewed-up jerky.*

But Dad kept chewing. "You've proven to me that you can keep yourself and your sister and Little Al out of trouble and that you can be responsible for making sure that Aunt Gussie gets a good rest. Don't start letting me down now."

"I can do it," Rudy said. *Now please, spit me out!*

One more good gnaw. "You used to be the one I worried about—the one who couldn't resist a good prank or a goofy scheme. Now I know what kind of maturity you're capable of, and Little Al and Hildy Helen aren't ready for that yet. Do you get my meaning?"

"I do," Rudy said.

Dad looked as if he were going to take a final bite, and Rudy held his breath. But Dad just took his hand from Rudy's shoulder and nodded. "I believe you," he said. "And I believe you'll be a man about this."

Then he put out his hand toward Rudy. Rudy stared at it blankly.

"Shake," Dad said.

Rudy put his hand into his father's palm and felt his warm grip. When Dad let go, he said, "You *are* my man, Rudy. Just remember what I expect of you."

"I will," Rudy said.

But as he watched his father make his way through the sand to the car, Rudy's mind whispered to him, *I think I would rather have had a hug.*

The three kids stood at the edge of the road waving until the pink Pierce Arrow was out of sight. Then Hildy Helen pounced on Rudy.

"Did Dad give you the business about the sand dune race?" she said.

"Yes, thanks to you," Rudy said. "Why'd you set me up?"

"Says who?" Little Al said indignantly.

"We didn't see them coming until it was too late," Hildy Helen said. "We screamed our heads off at you, but you couldn't hear us."

"Aw, forget it," Rudy said. He didn't have the energy to argue. Hauling around the weight Dad had just put on his shoulders didn't leave energy for much of anything else.

"So whadda ya wanna do?" Little Al said.

"We've already ridden all over Wellfleet—what there is of it," Hildy Helen said. "Bunch of apple stands and antique shops in people's barns. It kills me to think about Agnes Anne back in Chicago going to the Navy Pier without me and wearing her bathing suit down on the lake where everybody's there and—"

"It's not my fault!" Rudy said.

"Nobody said it was!"

"You two sound like a coupla squawkin' seagulls," Little Al said. "I'm gonna go off and find my own fun if you don't can it."

"No, don't do that," Rudy said quickly. "We'll think of something."

"Like what?" Hildy Helen said. "We can't do the stuff we like to do here the way we can in Chicago."

Rudy wanted to agree with her, but Dad's words were still nibbling at his brain. "Sure we can," he said. "What would we be doing if we were home on Prairie Avenue?"

Little Al shrugged. "I don't know. I'd be beatin' you two in hide-n-seek, maybe?"

"Exactly!" Rudy said. "Hide and seek in the dunes." He gave Hildy Helen a smack on the arm. "You're it!"

"Why do I have to be it?" Hildy Helen said.

"'Cause you're the girl. Now hide your eyes."

"Oh," Hildy Helen said. "Which means I'm smarter, which means it's more of a challenge for you to find good hiding places—"

"Just start counting," Rudy said. Hildy Helen babbled more the older she got. Sometimes she drove him nuts.

She finally did plaster her hands over her eyes and start counting out loud. Little Al disappeared before she got to "two," and Rudy scoped out the landscape for an escape of his own.

It wasn't easy hiding here, without many trees and only low blackberry bushes and tufts of grass. But if there was one thing Cape Cod had, it was ponds. Aunt Gussie had said there were something like 300 of them out here.

Rudy took off down a sandy path toward the closest one and picked out the perfect spot with his eyes. It would mean getting *into* the water, clothes and all, and ducking down behind a big hunk of wood that stuck up out of it, but it would be worth it to fool Hildy Helen.

I'm gonna hate being the boring one, he thought. *I gotta do what Dad said. But I gotta grab every chance I can not to be the bore around here!*

Barely making a splash as he slipped into the shallow pond—who *said* he wasn't athletic?—Rudy wriggled his way to the large piece of wood, which turned out to be a piece of a tree growing right up out of the pond. He eased himself into place behind it, just as Hildy Helen cried, "Ready or not, here I come!"

She wandered in the opposite direction at first, Rudy knew, even though he couldn't see her, because she was talking the entire time. "Don't think you can hide from me for long, you two," she was saying. "You forget that I have women's intuition, which means I can sense things that men can't—"

Rudy smirked to himself. She was leaving a yakking trail that was more obvious than bread crumbs.

Just then her voice pointed back in his direction, and Rudy held his breath so he wouldn't make so much as a ripple.

"I *know* you didn't hide in the pond, Rudy Hutchinson," she was saying. "You know what Quintonia'll do if you drown a pair of knickers."

Actually, Rudy *hadn't* thought of that, and he was considering whether this really was worth it after all, when he heard something besides Hildy Helen's voice. It was another car.

Rudy nearly groaned out loud. It was coming from the direction of town. If it was Dad coming back, he'd take one look at Rudy neck-deep in the pond with all his clothes on and say, "Is this being responsible, Rudy?" *Every time I try not to be the most boring person in the world, I end up in trouble!*

But the car didn't have the purr of the Pierce Arrow that old Sol kept running like a Swiss watch. This automobile roared as if it were angry, and its tires were spraying up shells so hard they were ticking and tapping against the sides of the vehicle. Old Sol would never allow that on Aunt Gussie's pink paint job.

Rudy couldn't stand it. He had to risk a peek around the soggy tree limb to get a glimpse of this machine that was barging in on the peace and quiet of Outer Cape Cod.

Just as he poked his head out, the car, a boxy black thing with tinted windows, dug its tire-claws into the shell road and turned sharply onto the sandy path that led straight to Rudy's pond.

For an awful moment, Rudy was sure the driver was going to steer it right in and take him down in its wake. But the car swung broadside of the pond and lurched to a stop. Its back door opened mechanically, as if someone had merely pressed a button to make it so.

Something in a large, cloth bag rolled out of the car, bounced dully on the sand, and continued on its way with a heavy splash into the water. Rudy was only vaguely aware of the black car gunning out of the sand and peeling out to the road again. His attention was frozen on the bag that was suddenly thrashing around in the water.

Whatever was in it was alive.

✠ ◆ ✠

Chapter Two

*R*u-dee!"

Hildy Helen's scream jerked Rudy out of his freeze and got him splashing across the pond toward the writhing bag.

"What is it?" she cried. "Do you think it's a shark? No, it's a barracuda. I know it's a barracuda—"

For someone who had been craving excitement only five minutes before, she was getting pretty close to hysteria. Rudy wasn't far behind her. His stomach had already turned inside out and was flopping around just like the bag was. Only a muffled sound from inside it kept him from throwing up right in the pond.

"Wep!" it said as if it were speaking through a wool stocking. "From—bede! Welp mrr!"

"It talks!" Hildy Helen cried.

By now she was at the edge of the pond, and Rudy had sloshed over to her, knickers full of water and hanging like cow udders down to his ankles. The bag was bulging, and Rudy saw now that there were elbows and knees in there. The way they were flailing, whoever was inside was going to drown for sure.

"Al, come here! Grab that end!" Rudy cried. "Let's drag it out of the water!"

There was no answer. Rudy groaned out loud as he squinted up into the dunes. "Aw, man! Where did he go?"

"We-eep!" the bag cried and did a flop that got it floundering in the worst panic yet.

"Come on!" Hildy Helen cried. She grabbed the other end, and the twins gave it a heave. Even with the two of them, it was a tough go to haul the bag full of person out of the pond. Once they did, it was still thrashing around so hard Hildy Helen finally had to sit on it so Rudy could work on the knot that was holding the bag closed. She was done with her near-fit and was already enjoying the first taste of adventure they'd had in over a month.

Rudy wasn't enjoying it. He glanced around anxiously again. *Dad's gone a half hour*, he thought, *and already I've lost Little Al and got some loony in a bag on my hands*. He gave the string a final tug and the knot came undone.

"Don't open it yet, Rudolpho!" It was Little Al, whipping around the dune, waving a big stick and breathing like an over-heated engine.

"Where have you been?" Rudy said.

"Chasin' the car, of course," Little Al said. "Too fast for me, though—and tinted windows. Those things shouldn't be allowed is what I say."

He shifted the piece of driftwood he was carrying to hold it in his hands like a sword.

"*Now* what are you doing?" Rudy said.

"I'm gettin' ready, case he lets loose. Anybody that's been shut up in a bag is liable to go crazy when he gets out."

Hildy Helen shot up like she'd just been poked. Rudy looked doubtfully at the untied string.

"Maybe we oughta just get the police or something," he said.

But just then the bag exploded with another "From-bede, welp mrr!"

"Sounds desperate," Little Al said. "We better let him out before he hurts himself, Rudolpho."

I hate being the responsible one! Rudy thought. But he pulled open the bag and started to cautiously peer inside. Suddenly the cloth was ripped out of his hand, and a head burst forth—skin red as a pepper, blond wiry hair sticking out in every direction as if the poor man had stuck his finger in an electrical socket. His ranting was still in muffled tones, because there was a white rag stuffed into his mouth, and he couldn't reach up and yank it out because his hands were tied behind his back, just as his feet were bound together at the ankles. Rudy went cold.

Little Al started to grab the gag, but Rudy snatched him back by the wrist.

"Let's just go get the police," he said.

"And let them have all the fun? Not on your life!" Hildy Helen said. The adventure-sparkle was bright in her brown eyes.

"Don't be a stupe, Hildy Helen," Rudy said. Couldn't she see that this man had been bound and gagged and stuffed in a bag and thrown into a pond so he would *drown*?

"Let's just see what he has to say," Little Al said, and before Rudy could stop him again he plucked the rag out of the man's mouth. The man went from, "Ged-dis-phig-off-mrr!" to "No police! No need for the police," without even taking a breath.

Then the man did take a breath, closed his eyes, and said, "Now, would you be so kind as to untie my hands?"

Nobody untied anything for a good 10 seconds. They were all staring at the man as if he were a circus act. In that instant he had gone from a madman to somebody's butler. The only person Rudy knew who talked that proper was their teacher, Miss Tibbs, and even she didn't have a voice that came out of her nose like it was a silver trumpet. What was a man like that doing tied up in a bag?

Little Al recovered first and went to work on the man's wrist ropes. Hildy Helen went for the ankles. Rudy watched uneasily.

"Nice duds," Little Al said, nodding at the man's very damp white suit, complete with wilted red carnation in the buttonhole. "Is that a real pearl in your tie stud?"

"What?" the man said. He glanced at his wet necktie as if he'd forgotten he was wearing it and shook his head. "I don't mean to be rude," he said, "but I really can't discuss my wardrobe right now. Do you have a car?"

Hildy Helen stood up from untying his ankles and handed him what at one time had probably been a handsome straw boater. It now resembled a soggy clump of white hay.

"Here's your hat," she said. "It must've fallen on the ground when you came out of the bag."

The man took it from her and positioned it over his startled blond hair. The brim flopped down over his forehead. "I say, do you have a car?" he said again.

"*We* don't," Rudy said carefully. "Our aunt does, but it's being used right now."

"Of course," said the man. He looked around, pulled the hat off and wrung it out, then stuck it back on his head. All the while, the children stood staring at him. It was like a scene out of a Charlie Chaplin movie, motions stiff and hurried, and Rudy was beginning to wonder if it were indeed real, when the man said, "I see you have bicycles. Could you do me a favor, then?"

"Sure!" Hildy Helen said.

Little Al wasn't far behind with a "You bet, fella."

Rudy gave a faint "Yeah, why not?" and then held his breath. He was doing a lot of that lately. Trying to keep everybody out of trouble seemed to require it.

"Does anyone have a pen?" the man said. "I usually carry one with me, but those scoundrels—" He stopped suddenly, coughed, and looked at them as if he expected all three of them to whip out fountain pens and begin taking dictation. "I must give you an address to deliver a message to," he said.

"We'll remember," Hildy Helen said. "We're good at that."

"Excellent," the man said. "Would you please go to Shoe Lane—there are no numbers out here—uncivilized as the devil if you ask me. But it's a gray house, white shutters, two-story with a widow's watch—"

"Oh!" Hildy Helen said. "That's right next—"

"And what do you want us to tell them?" Rudy burst in. He saved an are-you-an-idiot? look for Hildy Helen later.

"Tell them Louis is in need of assistance, and tell them where I am."

"We're not far from there," Hildy Helen said. "Why don't we just walk you there?"

The man's silvery-blond eyebrows shot up as if that were the most hideous suggestion he'd ever heard.

"Never mind," Rudy said. "We'll deliver the message."

"And that's *all* we're going to do," he whispered to Little Al and Hildy Helen as the three of them hurried to their bicycles. "This is trouble, and we can't be in it."

"Why wouldn't you even let me tell him the house he was talking about is right next door to the one we're staying in?" Hildy Helen said.

"Rudolpho was right about that, Dollface," Little Al said. "There's somethin' fishy about this whole thing. We don't need to be advertisin' where we live, if you know what I mean."

Hildy Helen hiked up her sailor frock and straddled her bike. "But I don't think it's *his* fault somebody threw him in the pond. He's not some thug or something—anybody can see that."

"Yeah, he sure talks like a sissy," Little Al said. "Nice duds, though. I always wanted me a white suit."

Rudy ignored the rest of the conversation and pumped his pedals to get ahead of them. The sooner they delivered this message for "Louis," the better. Maybe he could talk Little Al and Hildy Helen into building a sand castle or something. The thought was as boring to him as he knew it was going to be to them. But then, that was evidently his job now.

Hildy Helen, of course, passed him with ease on her bike, and led the five-minute way among the maze of small lanes lined with dunes and sea grass. Little Al got up on one knee on his seat and coasted down hilly little Shoe Lane toward the summer house.

"Wanna see if I can do a handstand on the handlebars, Rudolpho?" he shouted.

"No!" Rudy shouted back.

They pulled into the clam shell driveway of the gray house Louis had described and parked their bikes along the neat, white fence that surrounded a front yard riotous with lilacs. Unlike most of the summer houses where the inhabitants were there to vacation, not work in the garden, this yard looked as if it had been tended with manicure scissors. A well-trimmed hedge banked the front walk like the walls of a maze, and around the front door was an arbor dripping with cascades of bridal wreath flowers.

"This stuff makes me sneeze," Little Al said.

"Well, don't wipe your nose on your sleeve," Hildy Helen said. "These are high-class people, I can tell."

"Not any classier than Miss Gustavio!" Little Al said.

"Shh!"

The front door opened, and there stood a petite woman with hair so blonde it was almost white and styled in such neat Marcel waves, it looked like porcelain. Her green eyes had the same hand-painted look, and so did her china-white skin. Rudy expected that when she opened her mouth to speak, her cheeks were going to break out in tiny cracks.

"Yes?" she said. The face remained intact. The voice sounded a lot like Louis's, only hers was more flute-like. It still trailed properly out of her nostrils.

Hildy Helen stepped forward and put out her hand. "I'm Hildy Helen Hutchinson, your next door neighbor," she said. "Of course, we're only summer people here, but we're still neighbors. And we've come across a friend of yours—"

Rudy was ready to clap his hand over her mouth and haul her off. Little Al was giving her a deep scowl. But the woman smiled to reveal teeth as perfect as the long string of pearls which she fingered with tiny, well-polished hands.

"A friend of ours?" the woman said. "I'm afraid you must be mistaken. We're summer people, too, from Boston. We don't know anyone here."

"Now you know us!" Hildy Helen said brightly. "And this person knows you. He said his name is Louis. We found him in the oddest place—"

The pearls dropped and swayed nervously across the woman's chest. "Louis?" she said.

"Then you do know him!" Hildy Helen said. "We found him—"

"Where?" the woman said. The green eyes were now searching Hildy Helen's face as if it were a road map to someplace she desperately needed to be.

Rudy stepped in front of Hildy Helen and ignored her indignant grunt. "You go down to the bottom of our lane," he said, "and then go right, a couple blocks away from the ocean. You'll see a little path that leads to a pond."

"He's in a white suit—soakin' wet,' Little Al said. 'You can't miss him."

The woman was nodding, but the door was already closing. She all but said, "Thank you. Go away now!"

We can take a hint, Rudy thought.

He turned to give Hildy Helen a little shove down the walk.

"Thank you," the woman said abruptly.

"It was nothing, really," Hildy Helen said, and took a deep breath to launch into another paragraph. Rudy kept pushing her and looked over his shoulder to answer the lady. Just as he did, he caught a glimpse of someone else, just behind the woman. It was a girl, younger than the twins, and she looked exactly like the woman, only smaller. They were like a pair of those dolls Hildy Helen used to play with, the ones with the perfect faces—until the twins had painted on Indian war paint and Charlie Chaplin mustaches.

The woman seemed to notice the girl there at the exact moment Rudy did. She gave what sounded like a gasp and then snapped the door shut. The click of the handle was followed by several more clinks and snaps and boltings. There must have been five locks on the inside of that door.

But Rudy didn't have time to wonder why somebody needed to be bolted inside a house on boringly peaceful Outer Cape Cod. For from the other side of the door, a voice rose like a shrill, twittering flute.

"Marjorie!" it said. "I thought I told you to stay out of sight!"

✝ ✝ ✝

Chapter Three

"Now what was *that* all about?" Hildy Helen said. Rudy could practically see her ears standing up on end under her bob.

"Never mind," Rudy said, and he gave her another push.

"Would you quit shoving me?" she said. "You're getting to be such an old woman, Rudy!"

Fortunately for him—or maybe for her—another "old woman" called to them just then.

"Chil-dren!" Quintonia bellowed from the back porch of the summer house. "You better get yourselves home and shuck these oysters!"

Rudy broke into a run for his bike as if Quintonia had just invited them to exit town with the circus.

"What's so nifty about oysters?" he heard Hildy Helen say to Little Al.

"You gotta go easy on them artists, Dollface," Little Al said. "They got moods like a yo-yo."

Rudy knew this had nothing to do with being an artist or liking oysters. He just wanted to shift Hildy Helen's attention and get that adventure look out of her eyes. Whenever she got that look, it meant trouble.

Aunt Gussie was waiting on the back porch in a wooden rocking chair that she'd found in an antique barn the second day they'd been on the Cape and had already painted bright red.

"Contrary to popular belief," she had told the children, "our ancestors here in Massachusetts used a lot of bright colors. They didn't drag around all in black the way you see in the history books."

"Your father got these at the fish market this mornin' 'fore he left," Quintonia said now, pointing to the pail of oysters on the porch, "and they got to be shucked and eaten tonight, because the ice man hasn't come yet." She continued to mumble about what a load of trouble it was to uproot everything and come to this place for the summer when she had everything she needed in her kitchen in Chicago.

"I know what you mean, Quintonia," Hildy Helen said.

"Here," Rudy said, thrusting a blunt metal stick into her hand. "Shuck."

"Hey, Miss Gustavio," Little Al said.

"Yes, Alonzo," Aunt Gussie said.

Her voice was a little more brittle than it had been a year ago when Rudy and Hildy Helen and their father had first gone to Chicago from Indiana to live with her. But her eyes were still penpoint sharp behind her glasses, and she sat just as straight and tall and lean in her chair as she ever had—sort of like a judge who saw it all and didn't mind telling you just exactly what it was.

In fact, the only visible evidence that she'd had a stroke last winter was the elegantly carved, straight-from-Germany walking stick that was parked against the wall behind her chair. With that in hand, she could still stay way ahead of the twins and Little Al, in body and mind. That was exactly why Rudy was steering the subject away from the Louis incident.

She's not to get upset, Dad had said.

"Rudolph Hutchinson!" Quintonia said suddenly. She clanged a bucket to the floor in the midst of them and towered over Rudy, arms folded. "Why are you lookin' like a drowned rat?"

"Fell in a pond," Rudy said. *He pierced his eyes through Hildy Helen.* She gave an exaggerated yawn and went back to shucking. "I think oysters are the slimiest things on the planet," Rudy said quickly. "They remind me of that stuff you cough up when you have a bad cold."

"Rudolph, that will be enough disgusting talk," Aunt Gussie said mildly. "I suppose no amount of tutoring on my part is ever going to break you children of the manners you learned before you came to me."

"You already broke me, Miss Gustavio," Little Al said. "Look at this. I can eat one of these without even slurping out loud."

Little Al leaned back his head full of dark hair, opened his mouth, and let a raw oyster slide in.

"Ugh!" Hildy Helen said.

"I rest my case," Aunt Gussie said. "Quintonia, would you please turn on the radio? I'd like to hear the news."

"Me, too," Hildy Helen said. "Put on Walter Winchell."

Aunt Gussie tilted her head of gray Marcel waves. Rudy found himself noticing that they weren't as neat and perfect as the lady's next door. Aunt Gussie didn't plaster hers down here or bother with silk stockings or even wear her African ivory bracelets up to her elbows the way she did in Chicago.

"Since when are you so interested in what goes on in the world?" Aunt Gussie said to Hildy Helen. "I thought you'd be clamoring for Rudy Vallee."

"Since I came to a place where it feels like the whole rest of the world is going on without me," Hildy Helen said. She put in a dramatic sigh.

"Poor dear," Aunt Gussie said, voice dry. "That's precisely why so many writers come here. Did you know that Edna St. Vincent Millay has written poetry here? Or that Edmund Wilson, one of the great literary critics of this decade, has come here for long periods to write?"

Rudy knew that if she'd dared, Hildy Helen would have given another one of those cavernous yawns that read, "I am so bored!" She didn't, of course.

"I'm not a writer, Aunt Gussie," she said instead. "I'd rather be in the city."

"Nonsense," said Aunt Gussie. She deftly snapped open an oyster, slid the slippery meat into her bowl, and tossed the shell into a bucket.

"All our water's gonna taste like fish now," Quintonia mumbled. She opened the squeaky screen door, shaking her head. "Haulin' water in like some pioneer woman. Why we got to come here and get water out of some pipe in the ground when we got perfectly good runnin' water back in the city, I'll never know."

The door squeaked shut behind her, and the radio snapped on inside the house. Walter Winchell's breathless, rapid-fire voice snapped through the screens to the back porch. "Good evening, Mr. and Mrs. North and South America and all the ships at sea. Let's go to press!"

"I could listen to Walter Winchell all day," Aunt Gussie said. "Very few people these days have mastered the language the way he has."

Rudy thought of Louis and his silver-trumpet voice, and he groped for another subject before Hildy Helen could blurt out the whole thing.

"Listen!" he said. "He's talking about Sasquatch again!" *Thank goodness.*

"Another sighting of the big-footed monster has been reported from the Washington-Canada border today," Winchell said crisply as the ever-present code signal beeped in the background. "While only one witness actually saw the 10-foot-tall monster stalking through foggy Battle Falls, Washington, several claim to have seen his footprints and stood in them. Three men say they stood in one footprint, with room to spare."

"That is ridiculous," Aunt Gussie said, turning to face the screen door as if Walter Winchell were sitting on the other side. "I'm surprised a man of your caliber would even report such a thing." She went back to her oyster with her lips pursed. "Turn that off, would you, Quintonia?" she said. "Now you children listen to me."

Rudy suppressed a groan. Little Al looked at him, and Rudy knew he was hoping Rudy would make a joke or pretend the oyster he was currently prying open was attacking him or slide one of the slimy shellfish down Hildy Helen's back. But Rudy could hear Dad's voice, and worse, see the disappointed look in his eyes. He glued his own eyes to Aunt Gussie and tried to listen.

"Cheap thrills are all the rage now, I know that," she was saying. "And that is precisely why I brought you children here for the summer."

"We know, Aunt Gussie," Hildy Helen said. "Dad was just talking about that before he left. Did we tell you we met up with him on the road?"

"Go on, Aunt Gussie," Rudy said through his teeth.

"There is something about being on the ocean like this. It takes a person back to elemental things—a sea that can swallow you up, sand between your toes, wind in your face. Even the storms here remind me how vulnerable I am."

"What's 'vulnerable' mean?" Little Al said.

"Easily broken," she said.

Little Al's face opened up into his charmer smile. "That ain't you, Miss Gustavio," he said. "Ain't nothin' can break you, is what I say. Matter of fact, have I told you lately, I like an old doll like you? Tough, smart—"

Aunt Gussie's lips twitched, the way only Little Al could make them do. "What is it that you want from all this flattery, Alonzo?" she said.

"I'll tell you what *I* want," Hildy Helen said. "I want to know what we're supposed to do here besides wiggle our feet in the sand. I've already done that." She plunked an oyster shell into the bucket and stuck out her lower lip.

"I have some lovely plans, Hildegarde," Aunt Gussie said. "First of all, I want us all to be aware that, as I've told you, our Hutchinson ancestors started out in Massachusetts. They were among the original settlers. All their belongings have, of course, long since disappeared, but I would like to find some memento that will remind me of their start here. Who would like to go antique shopping with me?"

Goody, Rudy thought. He pretended to concentrate on a particularly stubborn oyster.

"And," she went on breezily, "I have brought along an old spyglass like the one your ancestor Josiah Hutchinson would have used on one of his ships. I'm displaying it on the mantel in the living room, but I think it will be interesting to actually use it—see the ocean the way our forefathers did. We may even sight some whales. Wellfleet was a big whaling town in its day."

"Uh-huh," Hildy Helen said with no tone in her voice.

"And since you aren't as fascinated with the sea as I had hoped you would be," Aunt Gussie went on, "I hope you'll like this idea: Clancy Faith is making a rare tour through New England and is going to hold a month-long revival right here on the Cape."

"Who's Clancy Faith?" Hildy Helen said. Her eyes lit up a little. "Is he a singer?"

"Sounds like a sissy to me with a name like that," Little Al said. He slipped another raw oyster slurplessly into his mouth.

"He's an evangelist," Aunt Gussie said. "He's part of the current movement to revive the Christian faith in this country. He has a reputation for being an amazing preacher."

"Oh," Little Al said, mouth dripping oyster slime. "So it's like listenin' to a sermon every night for a month?"

"You're kidding, aren't you?" Hildy Helen said. Rudy almost laughed out loud. Her face was as alarmed as if she'd just heard hair bobbing had been declared illegal.

"These aren't sermons, Alonzo," Aunt Gussie said. "This man pulls people out of their seats, inspires them to new heights, brings the Lord right into the tent where He becomes real to people who have been lost."

"That's a relief," Hildy Helen said. "I'm not lost, so I guess I don't need to go."

Jesus is already real to me, Rudy thought. He had been for a long time now, and Rudy had the drawings to prove it. Whenever Rudy prayed, he did it by drawing, almost as if he and Jesus were doing it together. It was a good friendship. Who needed a tent?

"Why he's coming to New England is anybody's guess," Aunt Gussie was saying, although it was obvious to Rudy that no one else was particularly listening. "These people up here are so reserved I sometimes wonder if they're all there."

"That lady next door is sure like that," Hildy Helen said.

Rudy nearly poked her with his oyster tool.

"You've met the woman next door?" Aunt Gussie said.

"Oh," Hildy Helen said, "well, kind of—" She looked warily at Rudy. But it was Little Al who saved her.

"We've seen her," he said. He motioned with an oyster shell toward the next door driveway. "There's some of her people now."

All heads bent to watch a pearl-gray Lincoln pull in, led by the greyhound ornament on the hood. The back door came open, and a man in a white suit which was plastered to his body got out, snapped the door shut smartly behind him, and walked toward the back gate with dignity—at least as much dignity as a person can have with pond water gushing from beneath his spats.

"Huh," Aunt Gussie said. "I guess the Potters have decided they need more domestic help for the summer. Looks as if this one ran into a mishap along the way."

Rudy started to give Hildy Helen a warning stare, but she was already giving him an "all right, I *know*" look. Little Al was innocently prying away at another oyster shell.

Rudy glanced across the yard again in time to see Louis being let in the back door. Even from here, with the ocean roaring in the background, Rudy thought he heard at least two locks clang and bolt.

"And," Aunt Gussie said as if there had been no interruption at all, "we have a visitor coming."

"Bridget?" Hildy Helen said.

"No, Bridget is up to her eyebrows in nursing school and helping to see after Kenneth."

Bridget was Aunt Gussie's former secretary who had shown such talent taking care of LaDonna's little brother, Kenneth, when he came down with sickle cell anemia that Aunt Gussie had sent her to nursing school in New York—and Kenneth to a special hospital there. Rudy was a little disappointed, too. Red-haired, high-spirited Bridget would add some life to this place.

"Your Great-uncle Jefferson is going to pay us a visit as soon as he can get away," Aunt Gussie said.

"Didn't we meet him at that family re-onion you took us to?" Little Al said.

"Re-*union*," Hildy Helen said. "I liked him! He hardly acted like a grown-up at all!"

"More's the pity," Aunt Gussie said, "seeing how the man is now 73 years old. It's time he *did* grow up. At any rate, he has an acting job in New York this summer, but he plans to take some time off and come here."

Rudy remembered Uncle Jefferson well. He drove a flashy car and wore outlandishly stylish clothes and made jokes about everything from the dusty Hutchinson ancestors to President Hoover's chubby jowls. Hildy Helen was right. Sometimes he acted younger than they did. Maybe that could be a good thing.

As long as I don't have to look after him, *too,* Rudy thought. He dropped another gray, lifeless oyster into the bowl and wondered if he was starting to look like one. He sure felt like one.

"I just have one more thing to say about all this talk of boredom," Aunt Gussie said. "If you are ever bored, you must always look inside yourself and see if it is perhaps you who are boring, not your circumstances. An interesting person is never bored."

It was probably the most depressing thing Rudy had heard all day.

Finishing the oyster shucking and then waiting for Quintonia to steam them and then eating them with heavy bread and fried potatoes seemed to take forever. It was dark by the time Rudy settled in with his sketch pad in the room he shared with Little Al and tried to pray.

He'd crumpled up four pieces of paper before he decided that everything he was drawing was about as interesting as Little Al's slow, even sleep-breathing.

It just looks like everything else I've drawn lately, Jesus, Rudy thought, and then he wadded up his current drawing, too, and tossed it in the corner with the rest. Although the air was much cooler now that the sun had gone down, the little upstairs room was suddenly stifling to him. He went to the window, wriggled through and dropped down onto the small dormer roof just below him. He and Little Al had discovered it the first night they'd been there. Little Al had said that in his old days back in Little Italy in Chicago, he would have found it a perfect place for smoking cigarettes. Tonight it was the perfect place to look at something besides his own boring self.

Rudy swept his eyes out over the ocean, but all he could see was mist. He only knew the sea was there because of its roar, its tireless roar.

But then there *was* a light fuzzing through it in faraway yellow.

Where's that coming from? he wondered.

"Hey, psst! Over here!" said a voice.

Rudy squinted in the direction of the sound. There, sitting on the roof of the Potters' house, was the little blonde girl.

✛ ❖ ✛

Chapter Four

*F*or a minute, Rudy wasn't sure she'd actually spoken. That is, until she cupped her hands around her mouth and called over the roar: "Meet me on the bluff."

"What?" Rudy said.

She pointed toward the ocean and then picked her way across the roof and disappeared through an attic window.

Rudy crept as close to the edge of his dormer roof as he could and peered down. Had she really said to meet her on the bluff?

She must have, for within minutes, a window near the back of the house opened and a stockinged leg appeared, and then another one, and the Potter girl lowered herself to the ground and looked impatiently up at Rudy.

Once more she cupped her hands around her mouth and said, "Are you coming or not?"

Rudy glanced up at the windows of his own house, half expecting to see Aunt Gussie glaring out at him. But the house itself seemed to have been lulled to sleep by the ocean's rocking. Rudy looked back at the girl and shrugged.

"Why not?" he said.

And why not? he thought as he scrambled back up to the window and got himself through. Little Al was still sleeping. *Everyone* was sleeping. What harm could there be in going down to the ocean? Aunt Gussie herself had said she wanted them to get closer to nature.

Besides, Rudy was sure if he didn't do something interesting in the next five minutes, he was going to bore himself to death.

It was foggy as Rudy made his way across the backyard to the gate which separated the summer house property from the bluff that hung over the beach below. The fog's misty fingers had started to reach in at dusk, and now he could feel them stroking his skin, clammy and cool. He kind of liked the feeling. What he wasn't crazy about was the fact that he could barely see in front of him. The bluff was 150 feet above the beach—a long way to fall if you missed a step.

But there was that light that came through it like a muted beam. It made the misty night just bright enough so that he could see where the cliff ended and nothingness began. Rudy crept toward it until he got another beacon—that voice again.

"Over here," the Potter girl called.

Rudy could make out her arm, waving to him out of the gray. He went to her, and when he got there, he found that she was sitting at the very edge, feet dangling over as if she were soaking them in a bucket of fog.

"This is a better place to sit than the roof," she said. "Nobody's going to poke their head out the window and yell at you. Plus I hate sitting on shingles. They make those awful patterns on your skin. And out here I can get rid of my stockings. Why my mother makes me wear them at the seashore, who knows? I took them off." She produced a handful of white stockings which she then proceeded to dump over the side of the cliff. "In fact," she said, "I'm going to mess up my hair, too."

With that, she put both hands to her very-blonde head and

scrubbed them through it as if she were giving herself a shampoo until it stood out all over her head in a fluffy yellow mass. Rudy watched in amazement, not sure which surprised him more: that she wasn't the porcelain doll he'd thought she was in the doorway or that she was the one person in the world who could apparently talk more than Hildy Helen could.

"What's your name?" she said.

"Rudy Hutchinson. You're Marjorie, right?"

The green-glass-colored eyes narrowed over her pert nose. It was so odd to see the placid doll's face suddenly go angry, Rudy wanted to back away from her—and would have if he'd known where he was going to land.

"How did you know that?" she said. "How did you know my name was Marjorie?"

"Because I heard that woman say it when she closed the door today."

"And who was that woman?" Marjorie said.

Rudy blinked at her. "How would I know? I guess she's your mother."

"Have you been spying on us?"

"What?" Rudy said. "No!"

"Well, I've been spying on you. You have a sister your age and a boy lives with you who couldn't be your brother because he isn't American—"

"Little Al is too American!" Rudy said. "And he is my brother. He's just adopted."

"Listen!" she said suddenly.

"To what?" Rudy said.

Instead of answering, Marjorie flopped herself down on her stomach and wriggled to the edge of the cliff until her elbows were almost hanging off. "To the ocean," she said.

"Yeah, what about it?" Rudy said. "It's noisy."

"That's how come people know you're summer people. Because

you don't know the ocean."

"What's to know?" Rudy said.

"Well, listen!" she said. Her voice was impatient, the way Quintonia's got when somebody spilled milk at the table. "Can't you hear it? There's always three big waves, then a bunch of little ones, then three big ones again."

"Oh," Rudy said.

"Shh! Listen!"

Rudy squatted down beside her, making sure he knew exactly where the edge was, and listened. At first, it was all just a roar, the one he'd wished several times that he could just switch off the way you did the radio.

But as he sat there poised, head inclined toward the water, he did hear it. One big, one big, one big—each one rolling in like a train on the El. Then four small ones, falling over each other like child-waves racing to see who could get to shore first. Then there was a crash that jolted Rudy back on his heels.

"That happens sometimes," Marjorie said. She pointed her face to the water again. "Show-off!" she yelled. "You just think you're the berries, don't you?"

"You talk to it?" Rudy said.

"It talks back. Hear that?"

Rudy listened, but all he heard besides the usual rolling was a faint hissing sound.

"SSSSSSS!" Marjorie said to it.

"What's it saying?" Rudy said.

But Marjorie was evidently tired of that conversation because she suddenly stuck her arms out at her sides and squirmed even farther to the edge—and out over the edge—until her whole chest was hanging out over nothing.

"What are you *doing*?" Rudy said. His hands got clammier and not with fog.

"I'm flying," Marjorie said. "They say we can't fly, and I say they're wrong. I know what it feels like."

She dipped her arms as if they were bird's wings. Her body rocked, and Rudy wanted to reach out and haul her back by the ankles. If Hildy Helen had pulled something like that, Rudy would haul her by the ankles all the way back to the *house*.

"Could you stop doing that?" Rudy said finally.

"You old fogey summer person!"

"You're a summer person, too!" Rudy said. "Your mother said so."

"Oh," Marjorie said. "She's an old fogey, too. Did you know that the only time she'll let me go down on the beach is in the afternoon when the whole beach is in shadow?"

Rudy shook his head. "Why?" he said.

"Because the bluffs are so high, they block out the sun from the west, silly."

Rudy didn't remind her that she was the one looking pretty silly, what with her hair all bushed out like some lion that was just getting its mane. "I meant why does she only let you down on the beach then?"

"Because no one else is there."

"Oh," Rudy said.

That didn't explain a thing, but it was all he was going to get, because Marjorie suddenly pulled herself back from bird position and got up on her knees. "Hey," she said, "how much would you give for some good penny candy? Do they have good penny candy where you come from?"

"In Chicago?" Rudy said. "Well, there's—"

"We have the best in Boston. Licorice that makes your mouth all juicy so it runs out the corners. Hey, have you ever smoked a cigar?"

"What?" Rudy said.

She didn't answer that question, either, but stood up, toes hanging over the cliff, turning Rudy's palms clammy again.

"Right now," Marjorie said, "we are ahead of the whole rest of the coast of North America."

"How?" Rudy said.

"We stick out. We're like a hand sticking out from the rest of the continent."

Rudy's head was spinning. "Where'd you learn that?"

"My governess."

"What's a governess?"

"My teacher at home, only she didn't come with us this summer. In fact, my mother fired her because—I don't know why. I didn't like her that much anyway. Mother wants to send me to boarding school, only I'm not going because then I'd *never* get to see my father." She stopped abruptly and then looked straight at Rudy. At least, she seemed to be looking at him, but her eyes didn't connect with his. They were those glass doll's eyes again. Rudy wanted to shiver.

"Let's go in the water and take turns pretending we're drowning."

"What?" Rudy said. "Uh, no."

"Are you afraid?"

Yes, he wanted to scream at her. Instead, he groped for another subject. She was good at jumping from one to another. Maybe that would divert her from leaping off the bluff completely.

"So Louis got here safely, I saw," Rudy said.

Marjorie's eyes flickered. "Who's Louis?" she said.

"I guess he's one of your servants or something," Rudy said. "Your new governess, maybe?"

"A boy governess? Are you loony?"

No, Rudy thought, *but I think* you *are!*

"I don't know who you're talking about," she said. "You're making it up."

"No, honest, I'm not," Rudy said. "That's why we came to your house today. He said to tell your mother to come get him. See, we saw this car pull up to one of the ponds and dump him into it in a bag. He had a gag in his mouth and his hands and feet were—"

"*You* are a liar!"

Rudy felt his mouth falling open.

"That did not happen!" she said. "I won't listen to you telling lies. I won't!"

Then she planted her hands over her ears and took off toward the houses. In seconds the fog had swallowed her up, and Rudy was left with three big waves, then three small ones, then three big ones again.

He decided right then that he liked the sound of the ocean after all. Anything was better than the rantings of a crazy girl!

I'm glad I made her mad, Rudy thought as he picked his way carefully through the fog back toward the house. *I don't think I could take too much more of her. It's like being on a merry-go-round too long.*

The air was still soupy, but that far-off light was helping. It was like a pale flare hitting once, then disappearing, then again, then again—just the way the big waves came in.

There's a rhythm to it all, Rudy thought. *Maybe I could paint it—*

But his thoughts stopped, and so did his feet. He could see the back of the summer house now, like a surprising discovery in the fog. And there on the back porch was a dark figure.

It was climbing in the back window.

✛ ⭕ ✛

Chapter Five

S uddenly Marjorie Potter faded into the past like a meaning-less dream. Rudy stared at the figure at the window, heart thundering.

Run! his head told him.

That was out of the question. His feet were planted in the sand, and they weren't moving.

Scream, then!

But even as he opened his mouth to do it, he knew it was use-less. Whether it had a rhythm or not, the ocean was still loud enough to drown out his voice.

And who would come anyway? Rudy thought frantically. *Dad's gone. Aunt Gussie can't—*

Aunt Gussie can't be upset. Rudy could hear his father saying it. That was the only thing that got his feet loose from the sand and took them through the back gate and toward the house.

Rudy was close enough now to see that whoever was attempt-ing to climb in the back window was having a hard time of it. That should give Rudy a chance to find something to bop him over the head with once he got close enough.

His heart was hammering, but so were his thoughts. *I gotta do this. Dad left me in charge. I gotta be responsible.*

By now the sound of his heart in his ears was even louder than the waves. He could barely hear his own thoughts shouting to him.

Find something! Find something quick!

The things we used to pry open the oysters—where are they?

By the pump. Quintonia took them out there with the buckets to clean them in the morning.

His thoughts were getting crazy, he knew. *I sound like Marjorie Potter!*

He rubbed his hands along the sides of his pajama legs as he crept toward the pump. He found one of the metal tools—by stepping on it. Forcing himself not to yelp, he picked it up and tiptoed in big leaps toward the house.

The person in the window was still having a rough go of it. Now Rudy could see that the window was open and that whoever it was had one leg in and one leg out. He or she looked almost crotchety, hopping on one foot and trying to maintain balance.

Rudy got an idea. He quickly stuck the oyster tool under his pajama top and poked it out like the barrel of a gun. Then, heart still pounding like a Congo drum, Rudy leaped up onto the porch. He had to do it now, or risk Aunt Gussie having another stroke right there in the summer house.

"Freeze right there!" Rudy said in his deepest voice. "Don't make another move. I got a gun."

The figure in the window flinched and tried to look around at him. There was a thud as a head hit the window frame. And then a deep voice cackled into the surprised silence.

"Couldn't you be a little more original, Rudolph?" its owner said.

It was Rudy's turn to flinch. "Who are you?" he said.

"You don't recognize your Uncle Jefferson?" the man said. "I'm devastated."

The man removed a straw boater from his head to reveal a head of white hair parted down the middle and shiny with pomade. Even in the dark, Rudy could see his tie, a loud, blue affair with white palm trees tossing on it in some imaginary wind. It was Uncle Jefferson, all right. Rudy pulled the "gun" out from under his pajama top.

"What is that you're trying to pass off as a weapon?" Uncle Jefferson said as he straightened the blue and white striped suit jacket that covered his wiry frame.

Rudy felt a little stupid as he tossed the oyster tool onto the porch table. "Nothin'," he said. "I just thought you were a burglar or something."

"I could never make a living at it," Uncle Jefferson said. He leaned down to brush off the pointy toes of his patent leather shoes. "Do you know how long I'd been trying to get through that window before you came along?"

"Why didn't you just go through the door?" Rudy said. He was starting to get wiggly with relief, and his voice was shaky.

"The door? What a concept!" Uncle Jefferson said. He smiled his impish smile—the one that reminded Rudy of a little boy who was up to no good—even though, as Aunt Gussie said, the man was 73. "I assumed they'd be locked."

Rudy gave a soft snort. "Not out here. Nothing happens out here. It's not like Chicago." The image of Louis being dumped into the pond in a bag flipped through his mind, but Rudy shoved that aside. That was such a freak thing, even Marjorie didn't believe it.

"Oh, well," Uncle Jefferson said. "It's always more fun to try to get in through the window anyway." He gave Rudy a wink. "You think there's anything to eat in that kitchen?"

Rudy grinned and led the way through the back porch door where he turned on the light in Quintonia's kitchen. She'd left it so spotless and shining after supper, Rudy hesitated to touch so much as a fork, but Uncle Jefferson started throwing open cupboards and inspecting boxes with a hungry eye.

Rudy watched him, mouth half open. There was nobody quite as bizarre as Uncle Jefferson. He was an actor, and Little Al said all actors were a little bit "fluky," which was what made them actors. Rudy wasn't sure about that. He just knew that one minute Uncle Jefferson could have tears in his eyes over some pet dog that had died years before, and then the next minute he could be telling you how glad he was that he was the black sheep of the family so that nobody expected much out of him. What Rudy expected was loud clothes and funny stories—and that was what he always got whenever Uncle Jefferson was around.

"Ah, chowder crackers," Uncle Jefferson said, peering at a box. "Can clam chowder be far away?" He opened the ice box and gave Rudy a disbelieving look. "What's this? An empty ice box in Quintonia Hutchinson's kitchen?"

"She hates it here," Rudy said. "The ice man hasn't come yet. She has to use buckets to draw water—"

"That's a pity," Uncle Jefferson said, though there was no sympathy in his voice. He grinned again and plucked out a can from a shelf. "Sardines. My favorite with chowder crackers. Will you join me?"

"Sure," Rudy said, and pulled up a chair to the table. Sardines weren't his favorite, but it was worth gagging down one or two to have some time alone with Uncle Jefferson.

A can opener was found, and Uncle Jefferson piled several sardines onto a plate and dug into them with relish, popping the occasional cracker into his mouth between bites.

"I'm absolutely famished," he said. "Do you know it's a five-hour drive from New York to here? And not a restaurant open after dark. It was absolutely uncivilized."

Rudy grunted.

"What does that mean?" Uncle Jefferson said.

"It's not very civilized here either," Rudy said. "Unless you like antique shopping."

"My baby sister," Uncle Jefferson said. "Do you know that Gussie is eight years younger than I am—and acts decades older, don't you agree?"

"I guess," Rudy said carefully.

"No wonder she likes antiques so much. She *is* one!" Uncle Jefferson cackled to himself and pushed the sardine plate toward Rudy. "Please, I hate to eat alone. Now, surely Gussie has other plans for you children this summer. Good heavens, you'll die of *ennui* the first week if you don't do something besides sniff ancient humidors."

"Does *ennui* mean boredom?" Rudy said.

"Right."

"Then I think that's what's gonna happen. She says we can look through the spyglass—"

"Yawn."

"Oh, and go to a revival, five nights in a row every week for a month."

Uncle Jefferson stopped with a forkful of sardine halfway to his mouth, and the wrinkles around his eyes crinkled. "A revival? You mean, a preaching type revival?"

"Yeah."

"The preacher wouldn't be Billy Sunday, would he?"

"No, I don't think that's the name."

"Pity," Uncle Jefferson said, shaking his head. "I hear he puts on quite a show. Stands up on the podium, gets people dancing in the aisles. It's a shame Aimee Semple McPherson disappeared. She was another one that could rock a revival tent. I hope this other preacher is half as good." Uncle Jefferson rubbed his hands together gleefully. "I can't wait."

"Why?" Rudy said.

"Because, Rudy, my boy, these outrageous people make excellent studies for future characters I might play onstage someday!"

Uncle Jefferson suddenly leaped from his chair, letting his fork clatter to the plate, and stuck one foot up onto the table. He put both arms up over his head and faced ceilingward as if he were about to address a company of angels.

"Lordy! Lordy!" he cried. "I can *feel* Your spirit in my soul!"

"Shh! Uncle Jefferson!" Rudy hissed to him. "You're gonna wake up Aunt Gussie!"

"Oh, and then there will be the devil to pay, won't there?" Uncle Jefferson said. He gave his most impish grin yet and pulled his foot off the table. "That's all right, Rudy, my boy. We're going to have a fine time anyway—or not."

"Not?" Rudy said.

"Not if your Aunt Gussie can get me to grow up this time, as she's been trying to do since she was 10, I assure you."

"Why would she want to do that?" Rudy said. "I like you the way you are."

"Let's just say my baby sister thinks that certain aspects of my life are not what they should be, and perhaps she's right."

He was still smiling, but for a moment there he looked like an *old* imp. It kept Rudy from asking what on earth Aunt Gussie could want to change about him.

Rudy was still thinking about that later, after the sardines had been consumed and the plate and fork washed and put away and Uncle Jefferson settled in on the living room couch. Rudy rolled into his own bed and lay staring up at the ceiling, imagining his uncle half standing on the table, imitating some hilarious preacher—while Rudy could only sit there with his mouth hanging open. *Being my boring self*, he thought. *I used to be interesting, I know I did, back when Hildy Helen and I used to always play pranks on people and all.*

He churned uncomfortably on the bed. *But I sure can't do that anymore. Dad would be so disappointed in me—and that would probably be worse than being dull for the rest of my life.*

Still, it was a depressing thought, one he would have done anything not to think about. So when he heard a car pulling into the driveway next door, he jumped up out of bed to peek out the window.

It was a Peerless. Little Al had pointed one out to him one day when they were riding bikes through the Northside of Chicago, where most of the wealthy had moved from Prairie Avenue. "They say they got all kinda fancy stuff in them cars," Little Al had told him. "Silver molding and velvet pillows with them little tassels on 'em. There's even a compartment for yer drivin' gloves."

It was too dark for Rudy to see inside the car, but he did see the man who unfolded himself from the driver's seat and closed the door behind him. He was a tall, thin man with a profile that cut handsomely into the fog.

The man started for the Potters' front door—rather than the back door the way Louis had gone in.

I hope either you have a really loud knock or you have a lot of keys, Rudy thought.

But there was no need for either one, for just then a figure bolted around the front corner of the house and jumped right up into the man's arms. Rudy didn't have to have Aunt Gussie's spyglass to know that it was Marjorie, and that she was about to burst right out of her skin, she was so happy to see this man.

Watch out, fella, Rudy thought. *In a minute she'll be asking you if you ever smoked a cigar or something!*

His eyes grew heavy then, and Rudy fell back down onto the bed. Three big waves crashed, then some smaller ones. Before the next set started, he was asleep.

He didn't know how many sets later it was when his eyes sprang open, and he sat straight up in bed. From out in back of the house, somebody was screaming her head off.

That somebody was Quintonia.

☩–☩–☩

Chapter Six

*L*ittle Al bolted out of the bed before Rudy could even get his
eyes all the way open, and the two of them tore down the
stairs, nearly mowing down Hildy Helen in the process. Uncle
Jefferson was headed out the back door in a sleeveless BVD under-
shirt and trousers, with dots of shaving cream still on his face.
Aunt Gussie was hot on his heels, or as hot as she could be with
her walking stick. She tapped Rudy with it and said, "See what's
happened to her, Rudolph. Quintonia doesn't just carry on for
nothing."

Quintonia had by now stopped "carrying on" and was just
standing next to the water pump with her hands over her mouth.

"Mercy, Quintonia," Uncle Jefferson said, "I expected to find
you half-eaten by wolves or something."

Quintonia pulled her hands from her face, but Rudy could tell
it was taking everything she had to calm herself down.

"I'm sorry, Mister Jefferson," she said. "I'm making a big fuss
over nothing. But when I saw it, it scared the living daylights out
of me for a minute there."

"What did?" Hildy Helen said. Even at that early hour her

sleep-crusty eyes were dancing at the prospect of adventure.

Quintonia pointed to the ground, and all eyes followed. By now, Aunt Gussie had managed to hobble out and join them, and she was the first to speak.

"What on earth made a footprint that size?" she said.

It was the biggest one Rudy had ever seen. There were two of them, actually, and they were cut cleanly into the heavy, wet sand, each toe and claw as clear as the foot itself.

"Sasquatch!" Hildy Helen cried.

"And how!" Little Al stuck his own foot over it and whistled. "I could put both my feet into that one print!"

"It's not as big as that one they were talking about on the radio," Hildy Helen said, "but it's still plenty big!"

"Oh, for heaven's sake," Aunt Gussie said. "I told you that was all utter nonsense."

"And you're right, too, Miss Gustavia," Quintonia said. Her voice was stern, as if she were scolding herself. "But, still—" She lifted her apron and fanned her face with it.

Hildy Helen scowled. "How do *you* explain it, then?"

"I say it was some giant bird that dropped in out of the sky," Uncle Jefferson said.

"Jefferson, really!" Aunt Gussie said. She gave him a poke with her walking stick.

"It makes sense, Baby Sister," he said. "You'll notice that there are only two footprints—none leading up to them." He gave his dry cackle. "Looks like a sky drop to me."

He was right, of course. Rudy glanced around him, but there wasn't another big footprint in sight.

"Sasquatch *is* a mysterious creature," Hildy Helen said. Her voice still held faint hope, but everyone else was already losing interest, especially Quintonia, who clucked her tongue and hurried off toward the kitchen muttering about being a nervous wreck having to live under these conditions.

Aunt Gussie suddenly looked at Uncle Jefferson. "Where did you come from?" she said.

"Got here last night," he said, winking at Rudy. "The night butler let me in."

"How did you get here?" Aunt Gussie said. "I could have sent Sol to pick you up at the station."

"No trains for this boy!" Uncle Jefferson said. "I just got myself a new flivver!"

"And what, pray tell, is a 'flivver'?" Aunt Gussie said.

"It's a *car*, Aunt Gussie," Hildy Helen said, rolling her eyes.

Little Al gave Uncle Jefferson's arm a tug. "So let's see it!"

Uncle Jefferson led the three children out to the front drive with Aunt Gussie bringing up the rear with her walking stick, shaking her head in disapproval.

"She thinks *I'm* frivolous?" Uncle Jefferson said to the children. "The woman who rides around in a *pink* Pierce Arrow."

Uncle Jefferson's new "gas buggy," as some people still called them, was a blue 1929 Model A Ford that made Little Al whistle in admiration.

"I like the color," Hildy Helen said, running her hand along the curved back fender.

"They call it 'Gunmetal Blue,'" Uncle Jefferson said. He hopped up spryly onto the running board and reached inside. The horns on the car's hood tooted like a pair of trumpets, making all three kids squeal with delight.

"Is this a roadster?" Rudy said.

"Yes, it is, Rudy, my boy. There's one seat for two people, and it's open air. That makes it a roadster."

"How on earth did you afford this, Jefferson?" Aunt Gussie said.

"It's called installment buying, Baby Sister. Don't you know it's old-fashioned to limit your purchases to how much cash you have on hand?"

"Old-fashioned and *smart*," Aunt Gussie said.

"Oh, Gussie, there's nothing wrong with exercising my credit on an easy payment plan."

"It isn't going to be so easy when our economy all comes crashing down."

Rudy looked nervously at Aunt Gussie to see if her neck veins were bulging yet—a sure sign that she was getting upset. "Will you take us for a ride, Uncle Jefferson?" he said.

"Just as soon as I've done my sunbathing," Uncle Jefferson said.

"*Sun*bathing?" said Little Al, who shrank away from the thought of *any* kind of bathing.

"Oh, come on, Alonzo, don't you know about sunbathing? It's all the rage."

"Then I want to do it," Hildy Helen said promptly. "How does it work?"

"Simplest thing you'll ever do," Uncle Jefferson said. "You put on your bathing suit, you stretch out on a blanket on the sand with the ocean singing to you, and you let the sun turn you a beautiful golden brown."

"I don't want brown skin, do I?" Hildy Helen said. She looked down at her very white arm.

"Of course you do! It's called a suntan. Everyone on the French Riviera has one, so who are you and I to be left out, right?"

"Jefferson," Aunt Gussie said, "I am appalled that you have completely bought into all this ridiculous advertising that says if you buy this car or get that suntan, you will be young, desirable, rich, the envy of everyone—"

"You're burning daylight, Gussie," Uncle Jefferson said. Rudy saw that his grin was that old-impish again, not quite as convincing as usual. But Hildy Helen's eyes were alive with something-new-to-do. Rudy groaned to himself. That took care of the two of them for the rest of the day. He turned to Little Al.

"Do you want to turn your skin brown?"

"Sure," Little Al said.

But the two boys lasted on the beach blanket for approximately 10 minutes. By then Uncle Jefferson was snoring, and Hildy Helen was determined not to get up until her skin was "a beautiful golden brown." She kept checking it every 30 seconds to see if it was happening yet.

"Come on, Rudolpho," Little Al said finally. "Let's go for a walk or somethin'."

The two boys left Uncle Jefferson and Hildy Helen lying face down on their respective blankets and wandered north up the beach. It was the first chance they'd had to inspect it carefully since they'd gotten there, and Rudy took it in with an artist's eye.

It was different seeing it from down here, 150 feet below the bluff where he'd sat just last night with Marjorie Potter. The beach itself went unbroken ahead of them for what looked like mile after mile. There was something so solitary about it that even in the naked glare of the gathering heat on the sand, Rudy felt himself shiver a little, and he dug his toes in deeper. The sand was yellow, almost brown, and warm and rich, and with his feet in it, he felt a little more a part of it.

As Rudy watched himself walk, he spotted some delicate bird footprints and looked up to find their source. A bevy of sandpipers skittered nervously off to the water's edge and let bits of ocean foam wash over their tiny feet.

"Those aren't like the footprints we saw this morning," Rudy said. "Now *that* was a big bird!"

"You don't think it was Sasquatch, Rudolpho?" Little Al said.

"Do you?"

"Nah. I'm thinkin' it was somebody up to no good."

Rudy looked at him sharply. "Like who?"

"I don't know. I ain't figured it out yet. I ain't figured this whole place out yet. I ain't never been someplace like this, y'know."

Rudy nodded.

"Like, what's all this stuff?"

Rudy watched as Little Al picked up a piece of driftwood and used it like tongs to scoop up a glob of sea lettuce that had washed up on shore.

"Some kind of seaweed or something," Rudy said.

"Smells like the fish market on Maxwell Street," Little Al said.

He poked the stick at a couple of empty sea urchin shells and a lobster buoy that had also come up with the surf, but he soon lost interest. They chased the sandpipers and some ringnecks for a few minutes, but that got old fast, too. Rudy occupied himself with checking out the colors and shapes of the plants on the dunes—the silvery green things, the goldenrod, and some others that looked like flat, green stars—when Little Al said, "Good idea, Rudolph. Let's go explore those dunes." He grinned. "But I figure one big pile a sand's pretty much like another."

It looked as if Little Al was right. The first two they climbed were, as he put it, "dead ringers" for the dunes they'd been playing in the day before. Sand you could sink into up to your knees almost. That silvery green grass that grew in clumps. Weeds that looked like peas sprouting up in unexpected places.

"They'd be a lot more fun if we could blow one up or somethin'," Little Al said, half to himself. "They just sit here."

"Yeah," Rudy said. "They're sunbathing."

Little Al grinned, then cocked his dark head at the next dune in front of them. "I got an idea," he said. "Whatta ya say we run up that one fast as we can, drop on our fannies at the top, and slide down the other side?"

Rudy considered that. It sounded safe enough. They'd get some sand in their knitted tank suits, but Quintonia would only raise Cain about that for a couple of minutes. There didn't seem to be anything about it that could upset Aunt Gussie, especially since their run was going to take them away from the ocean and down into a big bowl formed by several dunes. No chance of rolling into the sea or anything.

"Sure," Rudy said finally.

"Swell! I'll race ya!"

That would, of course, be no contest, since Little Al's sturdy legs always put him way out in front, but Rudy gave it his best shot, digging into the sand and pumping his arms like the rods that turn the wheels of a steam engine.

Little Al got to the top of the sand dune about eight steps ahead of Rudy, dropped to his seat, and, with a holler that sent two sandpipers into a running frenzy, disappeared down the other side. Rudy had barely reached the top himself when he heard Little Al's holler turn into a yelp of surprise.

Rudy sat down and scooted himself forward with his feet and went sailing down the other side of the dune, lurching and bumping over big silvery clumps.

It's worse on your tail than it is on a bike! he thought.

When he got to Little Al, however, he forgot the state of his bottom and stared. There, in front of his brother, was a large, wooden chest. It was battered, as if it had seen plenty of sea voyages, some of them rough. There were scars on its wooden sides, and the leather bands around it were worn and frayed.

"Holy smoke, Rudolpho!" Little Al said. "This looks like a treasure chest."

"It's a sea chest, all right," Rudy said. "I've seen them in the movies."

"How do ya think this got here?"

"You got me," Rudy said. He laughed. "Maybe Sasquatch brought it!"

But Little Al's face was serious. "I betcha this is somethin' important."

"How come?"

"'Cause look at this. Somebody took the trouble to lock it."

Rudy looked at the padlock Little Al pointed to. It wasn't rusty like the trunk's wooden corner pieces. In fact, as Little Al cradled it in his palm, it gleamed in the sun.

"D'ya s'pose it's treasure?" Little Al said, voice reverently quiet.

"I don't know," Rudy said. "What would it be doing here?"

"What's anything doin' here? It washed up on shore like everything else."

Rudy touched the chest. "It's not wet."

"'Course not! It's prob'ly been here—forever!"

That was a possibility. Nobody came down on this beach, as far as Rudy could tell, and the beach beyond them was even more like a desert. That sense of aloneness came over him again, and he tried not to shiver.

But the lock was new, at least newer than the chest itself.

"I say we try to get 'er open," Little Al said. He jumped up and began to ram around, looking for a tool.

"Uh, Al—" Rudy said. His insides were getting uneasy. "This thing isn't ours."

"It isn't anybody else's either," Little Al said. "Guy that owned this is long dead or he woulda come back and got it by now."

"I don't know. That's a pretty new lock—"

Little Al interrupted his search for a chest-opening instrument and got close to Rudy to examine his face with his sharp, dark, little eyes.

"What?" Rudy said. "Quit staring at me."

"I'm just lookin' to see where Rudolpho went," Little Al said. "Time was when you'da already had this thing half open by now."

A vision of Aunt Gussie watching them being loaded into a paddy wagon and then collapsing on the clam shell driveway flashed through Rudy's head. "I'm just not sure it's the right thing to do."

"Me either, boy," said a voice above them.

Their heads whipped back. At the top of the sand dune, on the ocean side, stood two men. Two big men. With fedoras pulled low over their eyes.

☩—☩—☩

Chapter Seven

*B*ig men who appeared out of nowhere with hats pulled over their faces was all Rudy and Little Al had to see. They'd had enough experience with thugs in Chicago to know there was only one thing to do, and that was run for their lives.

Little Al bolted for the up side of the next dune, and Rudy was only two steps behind him, when one of the men said pleasantly, "Hold on there! No need to run off! We're not the enemy!"

Little Al didn't even glance back as he took the dune in huge leaps. But Rudy hesitated and looked over his shoulder. Both men had made their way down into the "bowl," even in their polished blucher shoes, the fanciest around. They were smiling the way sales clerks did when you went into Marshall Fields to buy new shirts.

"Come on, Rudolpho!" Little Al cried.

But the taller of the two men laughed and set his tan fedora further back on his head. A shock of blond hair stuck out over his forehead, and his bright blue eyes twinkled merrily over a face full of freckles. This was no Chicago thug. And neither was the broad-shouldered man next to him who took off his hat to wipe the sweat from his brow, revealing sand-colored hair that was even curlier than Rudy's unruly mop. Even Little Al stopped at the top of the dune to take a second look.

"What have you found here, fellas?" said the tall man. He was wearing baggy oxfords, the kind of trousers Little Al had been dying to get for months. Sure enough, Little Al ventured down the dune to inspect them from several paces away.

It was worth thinking about the way they were dressed. Their clothes looked expensive, but they weren't flashy. Uncle Jefferson wouldn't have been impressed, anyway. Still, who wore flannel trousers and business shoes to walk in the sand dunes?

"Say, now," said the curly-headed one, "this looks like an antique sea trunk."

"Hot dog!" said Blondie. "I believe you're right."

Curly ran a hand admiringly over the top of it. "She's a beauty, isn't she?"

"She is," Little Al said. "And we found her first."

Al was grinning his charmer grin, but his voice was firm, and he was holding up his chin, the way he did when he was thinking there might be a fight in the near future. Rudy cleared his throat uneasily.

"It isn't yours, is it?" Rudy said.

"I wish we could say it was," Curly said. He squinted at one of the rusted metal corner pieces. "Vintage—oh—1790, I'd say."

"1790!" Rudy said.

"Definitely before our time." Blondie chuckled. "Looks like none of us can claim it."

"Yeah, well, where we come from," Little Al said, "finders keepers, if ya know what I mean."

"Oh, I certainly know what you mean," Curly said. "But tell me, what were you planning on doing with this treasure? It *is* a treasure, you know—the age of it, the condition it's in. Think of the history behind it."

Little Al surveyed the curly-headed man shrewdly. He hadn't been brought up in Little Italy for nothing.

"Why do you ask?" he said.

Blondie crouched down beside the trunk, and Little Al crouched protectively next to him.

Come on, Al, Rudy thought. *These are grown-ups. Let's just leave the trunk here.*

But Little Al obviously had no intention of doing anything of the kind. He rested his elbow on it and watched Blondie.

"We overheard you fellas discussing the situation," the blond man said. "From what I can gather, you're planning to try to get this open." His blue eyes were sizzling happily as he squinted against the sun. "I can't say as I blame you. What do you want to bet some pirate hid his ill-gotten booty in there?"

Rudy nearly groaned out loud. That was all Little Al needed to hear.

"That's exactly what I'm bettin'," Little Al said. "Now, if you'll excuse us, me and my brother here are gonna take this baby home, and we're gonna cut off this lock."

Curly suddenly yelped as if someone had stomped on his toe.

"Whatsa matter with him?" Little Al said.

"If you cut that lock off," Curly said, voice mournful, "you're going to deface it. You'll diminish its historical value."

"Well, no offense or nothin'," Little Al said, "but I've about had it with historical value. Ain't you, Rudolpho?"

"Sure," Rudy said, "but—"

"All right," Curly said quickly. "I understand. I was a boy once myself. But I do have a suggestion that will make us *all* happy."

Little Al's eyes narrowed. "What's that?"

"Let us take the chest to an antique dealer in Provincetown and have him get the trunk open. He's a professional. He'll be able to do it without ruining it in any way."

Little Al let out a huge guffaw, and Rudy grunted.

Even I can see through this! Rudy thought.

"Whatta ya think, I was born yesterday or somethin'?" Little Al said. "If we let you take this trunk, we'll never see it again."

Both Curly and Blondie seemed stung. They looked at each other with round eyes and then turned back to the boys.

"Oh," said Blondie. "I suppose I can see how you would think that way."

"How else would I think?" Little Al said. "Everybody's got a scam these days."

"I see." Curly's eyes were serious. "I guess they think differently where you come from. Here on the Cape, we're far more interested in preserving the property of our ancestry than we are in having a—what did you call it?"

"Don't tell me you don't know what a scam is," Little Al said. "You fellas are nothin' but a coupla oil merchants, is what I say."

"No, we don't deal in oil," said Curly. "We collect antiques."

Rudy let out a grunt. *Even I know an oil merchant's just a smooth-talking swindler.*

"You collect antiques out here on the beach?" Little Al said. "I know I don't come off all that smart, but you're insultin' Rudolpho here's intelligence!"

"We've actually found several fine pieces in the dunes," Curly said. He looked at his friend. "Tell him about that wonderful old mast we discovered down near Cheatham."

Blondie flashed a smile full of white teeth. "My brother here made me install it in the backyard. Our whole garden now looks like a shipyard. There's that anchor we found off Nantucket—"

"Oh, and the ship's wheel in Hyannis Port, although that wasn't completely intact. That was a pity."

"All right, so you got some kinda deal in mind?" Little Al said.

Rudy poked him. All they needed was for Aunt Gussie to find out they were making "deals" with strangers. He was really starting to hate being the responsible one. He was feeling more boring by the minute.

"No deal," Blondie said, blinking his blue eyes. "I just don't want to see a fine piece like this ruined."

"If you don't *want* it, of course," Curly put in, "we'll be happy to buy it from you. But you are welcome to whatever is inside."

"Wouldn't whatever is inside be antique, too?" Rudy said.

"We only collect large pieces," Curly said. "Jewelry doesn't interest us, naturally."

"Yeah, but what about the money you could get for it?" Little Al said. "And what if there's money *in* it—gold pieces or somethin'?"

The two men smiled at each other, as if Little Al had just said something little-boy cute.

"To use your term," said Curly, "'no offense,' but we really have all the money we need. Whatever is in this trunk would mean very little to us."

"Did you make a killing on the stock market or something?" Rudy said. He didn't add that they ought to be careful, that Dad and Aunt Gussie were sure that was all going to come crashing down on people any minute now.

"We've been very fortunate," Curly said.

"Besides," Blondie said, "as long as I can stay in oxford bags and good-quality bluchers, what else do I need, right?"

"Sure," Rudy said, before Little Al could get caught up in their mutual love for up-to-the-minute clothes.

"So do we have a deal?" Curly said.

"How do we know you're not gonna skip town with the goods?" Little Al said, eyes narrowed again.

The two men looked at each other again, faces puzzled.

"How do we do this?" Blondie said.

"I don't know. I'm not accustomed to making deals of this nature." Curly took off his hat again and ran his hand through his curls in thought. "All right," he said finally, "here's what we'll do.

We'll exchange names and telephone numbers. When we've gotten the chest open and have determined its worth, we will call you and return the entire thing to you, with the agreement that if you are going to sell it, we get first bid."

"If you don't hear from us in two days—" Blondie said. He looked at Curly. "What—they can call us, right?"

"Absolutely," Curly said. "Does anyone have a pencil?"

Sure, I always carry one in my swimming suit, Rudy thought.

Curly produced a little gold pencil and a small pad of paper in a red leather case with gold engraved trim. Little Al let out a long whistle.

"What are your names?" Curly said.

"Rudy and Al," Rudy said quickly.

"Last names?"

"Just ask for Rudy and Al." Rudy was already imagining the questions when Quintonia answered the phone. Somehow it didn't feel right to give them their last name, too. He rattled off the number and then took the small business card Curly handed him.

Kelly Brothers Antiques it said in silver print. The rest was so curlicued Rudy could barely read it.

"Has it got the phone number on it?" Little Al said.

Rudy nodded.

"You'll be hearin' from us if we don't get a call in two days," Little Al said. "And you might wanna keep in mind—our old man is a lawyer. And one o' the best, too."

Rudy grabbed Little Al by the arm. "We gotta be going," he said.

"We ain't settled this deal yet!" Little Al wrenched himself from Rudy's grasp and faced the Kelly brothers again. "What if we *don't* wanna do this? What if we just wanna take the chest right now and cut the lock off ourselves and too bad about history?"

Rudy's heart began to hammer. This sounded like trouble. Couldn't they go an hour without *some* kind of trouble?

"We'll just have to let it go, of course," Curly said. He looked sadly at the trunk. Even his curls seemed to droop. "After all, you did find it first."

He and his brother both shrugged. Little Al watched them carefully. Rudy died a thousand deaths.

Let 'em have it, Al. And let's get out of here!

"Whattaya say, Rudolpho?" Little Al said.

"It's a deal," Rudy said. Once again he grabbed Little Al's arm, and this time he didn't let go until they had reached the other side of the dune.

"Hey!" Little Al said, yanking his arm away. "Whatsa matter, Rudolpho?"

"I don't know," Rudy said. "I just wanted to get out of there."

Little Al shook his head. "Y'know, if we hadn'ta spent so much time talkin' about it before they got there, we coulda took the chest without all this havin' to happen. If ya don't mind my sayin' so, there was a time when you woulda been right there with me, tearin' open that trunk without even thinkin' about it."

He stopped there, but Rudy could see there was more he wanted to say. The words, *"You sure was a lot more interesting back then"* were clear in his eyes.

I think I was, too, Rudy thought. He shrugged and started back toward the house. "It's probably lunch time," he said.

When they arrived in the kitchen, Quintonia was just ladling out the homemade clam chowder into bowls, to Uncle Jefferson's obvious delight.

"Nobody cooks like you do, Quin'," he said. "Look at those clams. You haven't overcooked them and made them rubbery. I've had clam chowder that chewed like it was full of pencil erasers."

"You haven't tasted her scalloped oysters or her oyster stew," Aunt Gussie said. "Oh, and by the way, let's not forget to pick up some fresh peas from that little truck farm—"

"Could we please not talk about food anymore?"

They all looked at Hildy Helen. She was sitting at her place at the kitchen table, but her head was sinking lower than the bowl of seashells in the center.

"What's the matter?" Quintonia said.

"I feel sick," Hildy Helen said.

Aunt Gussie reached over and put a hand on her forehead. "Heavenly days, you are burning up!"

"Her face is pretty red," Rudy said.

"That isn't all that's red!" By now Quintonia was doing a full inspection of Hildy Helen. "Look at these arms!" she said. "And her back! Look for bites. Some sea animal has bit her for sure."

"Would everyone just calm down," Uncle Jefferson said. "Hildy has a sunburn—something you ladies of the Victorian era wouldn't recognize since you went to great lengths to maintain your lily white skin. Well, not you, Quintonia—"

"He's right," Aunt Gussie said. "These are first-degree burns!"

"I thought I was supposed to turn golden brown!" Hildy Helen wailed.

"You were." Uncle Jefferson looked down at his leathery arm. "I did."

"And you look like a piece of luggage," Aunt Gussie said. "I should never have allowed this. I don't care *what* they're doing on the French Riviera. We're going to have to treat this right away."

"I'll do it!" Rudy said. The veins in Aunt Gussie's neck were starting to bulge.

"She'll need a tepid bath."

"No, you *won't* do it!" Hildy Helen said, glaring at Rudy.

"I'll do it," Quintonia said, and *she* glared at Uncle Jefferson.

He picked up his soup bowl and said, "I think I'll eat lunch on the front porch. I have a stack of *True Confessions* magazines I want to catch up on."

Aunt Gussie clucked her tongue, but at least her veins went back down to their normal size. Rudy spent the rest of the meal praying that Little Al wouldn't bring up their "deal" with the Kelly brothers and get them bulging again.

When lunch was over, Aunt Gussie went upstairs to check on Hildy Helen and take a nap herself, which left Rudy and Little Al to their own devices. Rudy sure hoped Little Al wasn't depending on him to think of something to do. Rudy was feeling decidedly uninteresting.

"I know what let's do," Little Al said as they squeaked out the back screen door. "Let's go have another look at them footprints."

Rudy felt immediately uneasy, but he shrugged and said, "Sure."

"They're still here," Little Al said when they reached the pump. "But there's gotta be more."

"That's what Uncle Jefferson said. Unless the thing fell out of the sky."

"Let's look. You take that side o' the yard, and I'll take this one."

Rudy nodded and walked slowly toward the side where a flimsy fence cut the yard off just above a little slope, below which was the Potters' driveway. There weren't many houses in this part of the Cape, but these two were set close together.

They weren't much alike, though. The one where Marjorie lived was freshly painted and had green shutters, and of course the elaborate gardens everywhere.

The one Aunt Gussie was renting was a battered gray which hadn't been painted in quite some time. Several of the faded black shutters were falling off, and the back porch had what Aunt Gussie called a "romantic sag." She'd fallen in love with it the moment they saw it, going on about how it had character and was interesting.

Even some dumb house is more interesting than me, Rudy thought.

He tried to focus on the task at hand—finding more Sasquatch footprints. Drilling his eyes into the ground, he walked slowly, but the ground was too sandy here to hold any kind of print.

Until he got to the fence. Then there were several, but they definitely weren't those of a big-footed monster. In the moist, sandy area just on his side of the fence were some small prints, too big to have been made by any animals of the night around here. Especially since animals of the night didn't wear shoes.

"Hey, Al," Rudy whispered hoarsely. No sense getting Quintonia out here.

Little Al hurried over and looked where Rudy was pointing. He let out one of his low whistles.

"I told you somebody was up to no good," Little Al said. "But I sure wouldn'ta pegged Hildy Helen for that."

"Hildy Helen!"

Little Al jabbed a finger toward the ground. "Those are girls' prints. You know any boys step that light—or wear shoes with pointy toes?"

"Uncle Jefferson wears pointy-toed shoes. And he did try to climb in the window last night. Maybe he climbed the fence, too. I didn't ask him."

"Nah, these are too small for him."

"But Hildy Helen hasn't had shoes on since we got here!" Rudy said.

"It's gotta be her. What other girls are around here?"

"Oh," Rudy said. *"Her."*

"What 'her'?"

"You remember that girl inside the house over there—the one we saw before that lady shut the door?"

"Yeah," Little Al said.

"Her," Rudy said.

Then he told Little Al about his meeting with Marjorie on the bluff. When he was finished, Little Al hit himself in the forehead with the heel of his hand.

"It had to be her, then," he said. "If she's as blooey as you say she is, she'd probably do somethin' like that, just to scare the day-lights outta people."

"And how," Rudy said.

"Well, she isn't gonna do it anymore."

Little Al suddenly hit the ground on his belly.

"What are you doing?" Rudy said as Little Al wriggled under the fence.

"We're gonna go over there and give her what for!"

"No, we can't!" Rudy said, scrambling after him.

"You want all the women in the house to go blooey them-selves?" Little Al said over his shoulder.

No, Rudy definitely didn't want that, especially not Aunt Gussie. Maybe one little warning visit to Marjorie wouldn't hurt—if they could get any sense out of her.

And then Rudy remembered something. By now they were almost to the Potters' front door, and Little Al was walking with that swagger he got when he had a mission.

"She says her mom wants her out of sight all the time," Rudy whispered to him. "We probably won't even get to see her."

"Aw, I can sweet-talk that lady came to the door yesterday," Little Al said, swaggering even more. He cocked his wrist to knock smartly and then winked at Rudy.

But it wasn't the classy lady with the porcelain hair who opened the door. It was a tall, distinguished-looking man who was even more handsome in the daylight than he was in the dark.

☩ ⬦ ☩

Chapter Eight

*W*ell, good afternoon, gentlemen!" the tall man said.

His voice reminded Rudy of a clarinet, sort of low and reedy. He had high cheekbones and a finely chiseled nose, and his eyes were the pleasing color of a chocolate phosphate.

"What can I do for you?"

His greeting was so different from that of the china-haired lady, Rudy could only stare at him. Little Al, on the other hand, stuck his hand right out and engaged in a buddy-like handshake with the tall man.

"I'm Alonzo Delgado Hutchinson," he said. "And this is my brother, Rudy."

"Pleased to meet you both. You live next door, then?"

"For the summer we do," Rudy said. It was hard not to talk to this man, he was so pleasant and friendly.

"Then I imagine it isn't me you want but Margie, eh?"

"Margie?" Rudy said.

"Yes, but my dad's the only one who's allowed to call me that."

Rudy stared again as Marjorie Potter appeared in the foyer and wrapped her arm around the tall man's long, linen-trousered leg. It was exactly the sort of thing he would have expected her to say, but not how he would have predicted she'd say it. Her voice, too, was as smooth as a bowl of cream, and she was smiling two well-defined dimples into her cheeks. Rudy *had* to stare to make sure this was the same person who had set his head spinning on the bluff last night.

Little Al, too, was staring—at Rudy.

"Uh, yes, sir," Rudy said, "we did come looking for Marjorie." He looked at Little Al. "I think."

"I've just been introduced to your friends," the man said.

"Rudy is my friend," she said, causing Rudy's chin to drop to his chest. "But I don't know—"

She blinked politely at Little Al, who stuck his hand out to her, too, and shook, still gaping.

"And this is my father," she said.

"Sanford Potter," said the man. "My friends call me Sandy. Why don't you fellows call me Mr. Sandy, eh?"

"Nice to make yer acquaintance, Mr. Sandy," Little Al said. "The reason we come over here today—"

"Of course, you children have playing to do. I understand." Mr. Sandy slipped his arm around Marjorie's shoulder. "I'm so glad there are people Margie's age to play with."

"Excuse me!"

Another figure joined the ever-growing group in the Potters' foyer. Rudy couldn't help but stiffen when he saw that it was Marjorie's mother, the lady with the perfect, porcelain hair. She was wearing lime green silk lounging pajamas, but she looked anything but relaxed. Her face was as tight as a jar lid.

"Vivian!" Mr. Sandy said. "You didn't tell me Margie had made some pals."

"I didn't know she had," said Mrs. Potter. She was making no attempt to disguise her concern this time. She was looking so hard at her husband, Rudy was surprised he didn't crack in two.

"Marjorie, up to your room, please."

"Why does she have to—"

"Now, please!"

Marjorie looked up at her father, who nodded softly at her. She gave the boys a long, reluctant look and then disappeared. Mr. Sandy broke into an easy smile.

"I suppose that's that for today then, fellows," he said in his clarinet voice. "You know how it is when the lady of the house puts her foot down."

"Good-bye," Mrs. Potter said. And then she all but slammed the door in their faces.

They both stood staring at the doorknob for a good 15 seconds.

"That's one cranky lady," Little Al said. "We didn't even have a chance to ask about them footprints."

Rudy led the way down the front steps. "If we'd done that, her mother probably would have snatched us bald-headed or something."

"There's somethin' I don't get, Rudolpho."

"What?"

"You said that girl Marjorie acted crazy."

"She did last night! Today she was all peaches and cream."

"Huh," Little Al said. Then he shook his head. "Rudolpho, have you noticed that the older we get, the more confusing the dolls get?"

"Yeah," Rudy said.

But he couldn't just let it go at that, at least not in his head. There was something very strange about the Potter family.

Rudy and Little Al spent the rest of the afternoon combing the sand dunes for more treasure chests before the Kelly brothers could get their hands on them. They got so wrapped up in the search, they both forgot what was going to happen that evening— at least until they went back to the house for supper and found Uncle Jefferson dressed to go out.

"Holy mackerel!" Little Al said when he saw him.

Uncle Jefferson was wearing a double-breasted suit with wide, padded shoulders and a high waist on its jacket. The trousers were full and came up just as high on his jacket waist, and the whole ensemble was topped off with a matching hat.

That would have been fine, if the entire thing, except for the pointy-toed black patent leather shoes, hadn't been bright canary yellow, right down to the wide tie with the large sunflowers on it.

Little Al tried to whistle, but he broke off into a guffaw. Rudy couldn't keep the giggles from bubbling out of his own throat.

"What are *you* dressed for?" Rudy said.

"He *looks* like he's about to go to the circus," Quintonia said, clicking her tongue as she peered into the oven.

"No, Quin'!" Uncle Jefferson said, grinning his elfin grin, "I'm going to the revival!"

"Over my dead body," said Aunt Gussie.

She thumped into the kitchen on her walking stick, face drawn up like a prune. Rudy stuffed down his giggles.

"Divine!" Uncle Jefferson said. "We'll see if this old preacher's worth his salt. We'll bring him your dead body, and he can resurrect it!"

Aunt Gussie leaned on the back of a kitchen chair and pointed her walking stick at her brother. "In the first place, Clancy Faith is not old. The man's barely 35."

That sounded plenty old to Rudy, but he kept his mouth shut.

"And in the second place, he is not here to resurrect dead bodies. He's here to resurrect dead souls. For that, *you* are the prime candidate."

Rudy and Little Al both looked at Uncle Jefferson, ready for his snappy comeback. To Rudy's surprise, his uncle only stood blinking for a moment, as if he were trying to get something out of his eye. Finally the impish grin appeared, though it was that old-imp one again, the one that struck Rudy as being hard to get onto his face.

"You don't mean to tell me, Baby Sister," Uncle Jefferson said, "that this preacher's name is actually Clancy *Faith?*"

"I have no reason to doubt it," Aunt Gussie said. "Why would the man make up his name?"

"Well, Billy Sunday sure as heaven made up his. Nobody's last name is 'Sunday,' especially somebody that takes to the pulpit. That's just a little bit too much of a coincidence, don't you think?"

"I don't believe in coincidence," Aunt Gussie said, surveying him over the top rims of her glasses. "I believe in things being ordained by God."

Uncle Jefferson chuckled. "Do you think the fortunes these fellas are making are ordained by God, too? Shoot, if I had their gift for mesmerizing people, I'd sure do that instead of investing in the stock market."

"What does mesmerizin' mean?" Little Al said.

"Means they hypnotize people with their well-rehearsed carryings-on so that they think they've seen visions—"

"Jefferson." Aunt Gussie didn't raise her voice, but it was razor-sharp, and it cut right into Uncle Jefferson's words. "I will thank you not to cast aspersions on men of faith in the presence of the children."

"What's an 'aspersion'?" Little Al said.

Nobody answered him. Uncle Jefferson gave another dry chuckle.

"All right, Gussie, whatever you say. You pay the bills around here. Besides, I don't worry about Alonzo and Rudy." He winked in their direction. "They're smart boys. They'll figure it out."

"Figure what out?" Little Al said to Rudy as they went out to the pump to wash their hands for supper.

"Don't ask me," Rudy said. "I'm wondering the same thing myself. I think it has something to do with maybe this Clancy Faith fella being a phony."

Little Al sniffed. "I like Uncle Jefferson all right. He's a swell character and all. But I don't figure Miss Gustavio gets fooled too often. My money's on the preacher."

"Yeah, you're probably right," Rudy said.

"I'll tell ya one thing, though."

"Yeah, what's that?"

Little Al gave a grin so impish, for a second Rudy forgot that he wasn't actually related to Uncle Jefferson. "I sure wish I had a getup like his to wear to this shindig."

That was one wish Rudy didn't share. In fact, he secretly hoped Aunt Gussie had convinced his uncle by now to shed the canary costume and put on something that wasn't going to turn every eye toward them the minute they walked into the revival tent.

No such luck. Uncle Jefferson climbed into the Pierce Arrow with the rest of the family—minus Hildy Helen, who was still in so much pain all she could do was lie spread-eagle on her bed and moan—and he was still dressed in head-to-ankles yellow. Rudy groaned silently when he saw that even the socks were lemon-colored.

"Where did you *get* such ridiculous clothes?" Aunt Gussie said.

"I had them specially made," Uncle Jefferson said.

"Haven't you anything better to do with your money?" she said. "Or are you paying for these on the easy payment plan, too?"

"The answers are no and yes, respectively," Uncle Jefferson said, "though I wonder that you would have the nerve to ask, Gussie, since you squandered your money on a pink automobile."

"I had political reasons," she said.

Uncle Jefferson visibly shuddered. "Ugh, politics! Never touch them!"

"I know," Aunt Gussie said dryly. "Nor do you touch anything else that has meaning and substance."

"Meaning and substance," Uncle Jefferson said, snapping his fingers. "I knew there was something I forgot to pick up along the way."

Aunt Gussie shook her head. "I do not know how parents like ours could have raised such a son."

"Good luck, I suppose!" Uncle Jefferson said in a breezy voice. And then his face grew serious, just for a moment. "Perhaps it's you who had the good luck, Gussie," he said. "I don't know anyone with higher moral character, I truly don't." Then he threw back his pomaded head and laughed and said, "Thank heavens it isn't catching. I'm too old to start all over with a new life now!"

"Why would ya want to?" Little Al said. "You like yer life just fine, don'tcha?"

"Pos-a-lute-ly!" Uncle Jefferson said.

And then he immediately started to mimic what he thought the Reverend Clancy Faith would be like, waving his arms and shouting so loud even deaf old Sol seemed to hear him from the front seat.

The revival was being held up in Provincetown, at the tip of the fingers on the cupped hand that was Cape Cod. A good 20 miles north of Wellfleet, it was a much larger town with what seemed like 10 times as many people. However, only about a handful of them were in the big revival tent when the Hutchinsons went in and took their seats on wooden folded chairs.

"There ain't hardly nobody here," Little Al said.

"What did he expect, holding a revival for a bunch of stuffy old New Englanders?" Uncle Jefferson said with a chuckle.

"Stuffy old New Englanders are exactly the people who need to be revived," Aunt Gussie said.

A group of ladies on the front two rows of wooden folding chairs did seem excited about seeing Clancy Faith—and, it seemed, about his seeing *them*. They were dressed to the teeth, as Aunt Gussie put it, from patent pumps to silk hats, and they all primped excitedly as they chattered amongst themselves.

Others in the small crowd appeared to be merely curious. They sat in the back and whispered behind their hands and did a lot of giggling. When one of them let out a full-fledged snort, he was soundly smacked by his girlfriend, which brought on a new torrent of giggles.

And then there were the scattered few in the middle. They looked to Rudy like the out-and-out nonbelievers. One man sat with his arms folded across his chest, scowling at the front of the tent before Clancy Faith even came out. A couple, both clad in bright, flowing clothes like artists, took out pencils and pads as if they were going to write down all the ridiculous things the man said. A fourth person actually lit up a cigar and puffed arrogant smoke rings into the air.

Marjorie would like him, Rudy thought. He wondered again how she could have changed so drastically overnight from a half-crazy person to a normal little girl who had even looked happy to see him—and had referred to him as her "friend."

Maybe Little Al's right. Maybe it's just that girls get harder to figure out the older we get.

Just then, an organ suddenly burst forth in a trembling version of "Shall We Gather at the River." Aunt Gussie stood up, walking stick in hand, and so did all the ladies in the front two rows. Rudy looked around to see what everybody else was doing. To his relief, Uncle Jefferson just kept his seat and looked around.

Aunt Gussie gave Rudy a prune look, and Rudy at once took up singing. He didn't know the words, but he faked it pretty well with the help of the group of gospel singers dressed in long, gold choir robes who took their places at the front and led the pitiful little congregation. No sense getting Aunt Gussie all upset.

He was in the middle of making up the second verse when a flap at the front of the tent opened and a man appeared. All necks craned, even the cigar smoker's. The ladies in the front clasped the fronts of their frocks and looked as if they could barely go on singing.

Rudy had a little trouble himself. *Oh, brother*, he thought, *this fella has to be a fake. Either that—or he's just a loony!*

The man who stood facing them looked more like a movie star than a preacher. Although he wasn't much taller than Uncle Jefferson, he had a chest and arms like a circus strong man. They were visible even under the bright green, double-breasted suit. His face was perfect for the movie screen with its even features and bullet-straight eyes, and his honey-colored hair rose in two of those hills on either side of its center part in that way that always made Hildy Helen groan like a wounded duck in the theater seat next to him.

"What did I tell you, Rudolph?" Uncle Jefferson whispered to him. "Phony, through and through. Although I would like to know where he got that suit—"

The music faded, and Clancy Faith stood facing the gathered few and smiled a square smile that sent the ladies in the front to clasping their dresses.

"Good evening, my friends," he said.

There was nothing terribly remarkable about those words, but his voice was like a big wide door that swung open and invited everyone in.

"Great voice," Uncle Jefferson whispered. "Wonder where he took lessons."

Aunt Gussie shut him up with a look, but Uncle Jefferson still chuckled to himself.

"This is an intimate crowd here tonight," Clancy Faith said, looking around at the many empty chairs.

His loyal women in the front all sighed and looked terribly embarrassed, but Clancy Faith only smiled. It was a smile that went deeper than his voice. On the other side of him, Rudy saw Little Al begin to grin back at him.

"I have two things to say about that," said Clancy Faith. "One—" he held up a finger, and even it looked muscular.

"Those of you who have come out tonight despite the ridicule of your friends because of the so-called old-fashioned nature of my visit will receive an extra star in your crown when you arrive in heaven." Even from his seat in the middle, Rudy could see the man's eyes twinkling. They were deeply set into his face, but they had a shine that lit up the tent.

"What's the second thing you wanted to tell us, Reverend?" said one of the fun-pokers in the back. His friend snorted, and his girlfriend giggled. To Rudy's amazement, Clancy Faith snorted, too. The congregation roared—even the cigar smoker.

"I'm glad you asked!" Clancy Faith said. "The second thing—" Two meaty fingers went up. "The second thing I want to say is that our Lord Jesus Christ chose only 12 disciples to send out. And they were a motley crew if anybody ever saw one!"

"What does 'motley' mean?" Little Al whispered loudly.

Clancy Faith's eyes darted toward the Hutchinsons' row. "Excellent question!" Clancy Faith moved toward them, boring down on Al with his shiny bullet eyes. He was remarkably light on his feet. "Motley!" he cried. "A group composed of many contrasting people—so different from each other they could never possibly have anything in common. And yet under His teachings, they found just that thing: their love for God, their faith in Jesus' teachings, a whole new way to live!" His voice had risen, but now it plumped down softly on his next words. "And believe me, if there were ever men who needed a new way to live it was Peter and John and Matthew."

"And Judas!" somebody in the back barked.

Clancy Faith nodded sadly. "Poor Judas. Even Jesus didn't win them all over. But that was Judas's unfortunate choice, wasn't it?" His smile zinged around the tent. "I am so thankful that none of you made that choice tonight. Now let me ask you a question."

"Is this a test?" the snorter in the back said.

But several of the people who were sitting with him shushed

him up.

"No! This is a—let's call it a survey," the reverend said. "Because there are no wrong answers. How many of you are completely happy with your lives right now? Right this very minute? There is nothing you would want to change. Who can say that?"

Rudy held his breath, waiting for Uncle Jefferson's yellow arm to go shooting up. But his uncle sat perfectly still. In fact, no one in the tent raised his or her hand. It was as if they were all—what was that word?—mesmerized by Clancy Faith's eyes as he swept them over the small assembly. A hush fell in the tent, and Clancy Faith spoke into it with his open-door voice.

He told them about the lives of the disciples before they met Jesus—how some worked difficult jobs and some were criminals and some were practically outcasts from society. Didn't it sound a lot like now? Clancy wanted to know. Heads nodded around the tent.

So, Clancy said, they gave up everything that came between themselves and their happiness, and they started all over with Jesus. It wasn't easy. People told them they were idiots. Villagers ran them out of town. Officials who had the power to make their lives miserable threatened to do just that if they didn't abandon their teacher.

"But there wasn't a chance they were going to leave Him," Clancy said, voice dramatically quiet and deep. "He was teaching them how to live a life so rich, so abundant, they never need worry about happiness again, because it was theirs."

Clancy Faith looked down at his outstretched hands as if he were holding that life right there. Then he swept his eyes over his audience again. "I know this sounds like pie-in-the-sky-by-and-by. You've probably heard something similar from every salesman who has ever come to your front door. But no salesman could offer you what Jesus can, no matter what he's selling. *No* salesman can offer you peace of mind! Self-respect! The guarantee that you will *always, always* be taken care of! *No* salesman can promise you that you need never worry again about what other people think of you! *No* salesman is going to be there for you every minute of every day of your life, guiding you in the Way that is going to make you happy and peaceful and always at home. And *no* salesman, no matter who he works for, can guarantee you everlasting life." Clancy Faith paused. Then he held out his two magnificent, green-clad arms.

"But, my friends," he went on, "no matter who *you* are, Jesus Christ can offer you that. He promises that. He *guarantees* that. It's *yours*. All you have to do is cast aside your sins—all the things that are standing in the way of your true happiness, all the things that are separating you from God—and put your hand out for Jesus."

The room was alive with silence as Clancy Faith put out a beefy hand and closed his eyes. A look of pure peace settled over his features, and even behind his closed lids, Rudy could imagine his eyes shining. And then Clancy raised both of his mighty arms toward heaven and stood there, fingers outstretched, as if he were reaching. It suddenly occurred to Rudy that this was what Uncle Jefferson had predicted all along.

Rudy snickered inside his head. *When I get home, I'm gonna draw a comic of this character. Uncle Jefferson will get a kick out of that.*

He gave his uncle a gentle poke in the side with his elbow, but there was no response. Rudy glanced up at him. Uncle Jefferson was sitting at the edge of his folding chair, hands folded between his knees. He was watching Clancy Faith's every move, and there was no impish grin on his face. In fact, his shoulders were slumped, as if what the preacher had said had wilted him, like one of the sunflowers on his tie.

As Clancy Faith went on, claiming that Jesus Christ was right here in the tent with them tonight, just waiting to take every one of their problems on his shoulders, Rudy looked at the rest of his family.

Little Al was watching Clancy Faith as if he had just replaced Al Capone as his model for living.

Aunt Gussie was wiping her eyes.

Even old Sol had his hand cupped around his ear so he could hear better.

Rudy looked back at Clancy Faith and tried to listen again.

"There is no sin too big for our Lord Jesus to forgive," he was shouting. "No matter what your life has been like up until now, He wants you to come to Him and ask forgiveness and start over. Only this time, He's there to help you."

I know all that, Rudy thought. *I think about it every night when I'm drawing my prayers.*

Of course, it *had* been a little harder to do that lately, but that was only because it *was* the same old stuff. Once you learned it, it was just that way.

He looked again at Aunt Gussie. If anybody knew it all when it came to Christianity it was his aunt. But right now, she looked as if she were hearing it all for the first time, and it was moving her to tears. Hardly anything moved Aunt Gussie to tears. Rudy was just beginning to wonder if this might be too much for her, when Clancy Faith came right down to the middle of the congregation, stretched out his hands to both sides, and said:

"If there is anyone here who would like to come forward and give his or her life to Jesus, I am inviting him or her to do that right now. Is there any such person here?"

And then to Rudy's horror, Uncle Jefferson stood up next to him in his bright yellow suit, stretched out his hand toward the aisle, and said, "I would, Reverend Faith. I certainly would."

✟ ✟ ✟

Chapter Nine

*N*o, *don't do this!* Rudy wanted to shout. *This is too embarrassing! I'm gonna die here!*

It wasn't just the fact that Uncle Jefferson resembled a large banana and everyone in the tent was now focused on him. It was also the tears running down his uncle's cheeks and the hands raised heavenward and the look of ecstasy on his face, as if he were indeed seeing Jesus right there in the tent.

He really is a good actor, Rudy thought. But he didn't feel like applauding. He felt like crawling under the folding chair and expiring.

Instead he looked at Aunt Gussie, fully expecting her to be staring Uncle Jefferson down with her dart-pointy eyes. If anybody could break him out of this act, it was "Baby Sister."

Because of course Uncle Jefferson was acting, Rudy thought. He had to be. He'd said the only reason he was going to the revival was to study for new characters. He was, after all, a professional actor.

Still, though, Aunt Gussie didn't look angry at all. She was white-faced and watery-eyed and not saying a word.

Maybe, he decided, she was just too embarrassed to say or do anything. He didn't ever remember seeing her embarrassed before. Usually nobody dared do anything embarrassing in front of her.

"Look out, Rudolpho," Little Al whispered.

Al was motioning for Rudy to step back so Uncle Jefferson could get past him. Rudy watched with his chin hanging as his great-uncle made his way to the aisle and threw himself into Clancy Faith's big arms.

Oh, brother, Rudy thought. *He's giving the performance of his life.*

Uncle Jefferson was sobbing by now. Clancy Faith led him slowly up to the front of the tent where there was a small kneeling bench. Reverend Faith told Uncle Jefferson to kneel on it, and then he put his hands on Jefferson's head and began to pray—for all his sins to be forgiven, for Jesus to come into his heart and save him, for Uncle Jefferson to begin a whole new life, lived only for Jesus.

Jesus, You must be hating this! Rudy thought suddenly. At once, he felt sick to his stomach. It was one thing to make fun of a preacher in the privacy of your own kitchen, but to make fun of *Jesus* out here in front of everybody—in a yellow suit!—that was something else. Rudy thought his face was going to explode, it was so hot. He didn't dare look at anybody else, not even Little Al.

When the prayers were over and Uncle Jefferson stood up, the congregation clapped and hollered, the way they might have at the end of one of Uncle Jefferson's stage plays.

"Somebody ought to say 'Amen!'" Clancy Faith shouted.

The rest of the congregation hollered "Amen!" for what seemed to Rudy like a good five minutes. Rudy only stood there, hoping this thing was over.

It wasn't. It went on and on into the night—the Reverend Clancy refusing to stop until the sweat was pouring down his face and two more people had come forward to throw themselves on the mercy of the Lord.

And even then, the minute the meeting was finally finished and people started filing out of the tent, Uncle Jefferson grabbed both of Clancy Faith's hands and said, "You must come to our house for a late supper—I insist! You've saved my life tonight. It's the least we can do. Isn't that right, Gussie?"

"Certainly," Aunt Gussie said.

Rudy couldn't read anything in her voice. It wasn't angry or even disappointed. It was just calm.

She doesn't want to have a family fight in front of this fella, Rudy thought. *She's gonna wait and blow later.*

Rudy started to mention that to Little Al, but he was already introducing himself, charmer fashion, to the Reverend Faith and pumping his hand like a piston. Rudy wished Hildy Helen were there. She'd see exactly what was going on.

Whatever it was, Uncle Jefferson was determined to continue it at the summer house. He rode with Clancy Faith in his somewhat battered black Model T to make sure the preacher didn't get lost, and when they all arrived back in Wellfleet, after a very silent ride in the Pierce Arrow, Uncle Jefferson burst out of the car and started shouting menu suggestions at Quintonia, who was rocking on the front porch.

But it wasn't that which caught Rudy's attention. It was the two figures sitting on the roof above her.

One was Hildy Helen. The other was unmistakably Marjorie Potter.

"Uh, Aunt Gussie, watch your step," he said. With any luck he could keep her eyes to the ground until they got into the house. "If one of those shells is sticking up the wrong way, you could take a tumble."

Aunt Gussie gave her dry-leaf laugh. "Rudolph, there was a time when I would have suspected you of planting just such a shell in my path. Things are changing all the time." She looked at Uncle Jefferson, who was bending Clancy Faith's ear all the way up the steps, hands flailing excitedly.

"You really think—" Rudy started to say to his aunt.

But Aunt Gussie hobbled on toward the house with her eyes on her brother. At least that kept her from looking up at the roof. When Rudy did, he saw that the girls had disappeared.

And when he got up to Hildy Helen's room, she was lying in the same position she'd been in when they'd left, eyes closed, breathing evenly.

"Faker," Rudy said to her. "I saw you up on the roof."

Her eyes flew open. "Did anybody else?"

"No, thanks to me. You can pay me later."

"You can pay *me* later! Why didn't you tell me we had such a nice girl staying right next door?"

"I didn't know she was a nice girl!"

"And you call *me* a faker! She said she met you last night and that she really liked you."

"She did not say that!" Rudy said.

"Well, she most certainly did!" Hildy Helen bent her arms to put her hands on her hips, and then whimpered. "Ouch! This hurts so bad, Rudy."

"Sorry." He sniffed. "What smells?"

"Vinegar. Quintonia made me put it on to take the sting out— and it doesn't even help that much."

"Then you might wanna wash it off before you come downstairs. We have company."

"You could just tell Aunt Gussie I was asleep and you didn't want to wake me."

"No, because—"

"I know, because that isn't the truth and you're Mr. Honest now. I know." Hildy Helen rolled her eyes. "So who's down there?"

Rudy told her, and he also told her what had happened at the revival. The more he talked, the rounder her brown eyes got. When he was finished, her mouth was round, too.

"Rats! I wish I'd been there!" she said.

"Me, too," Rudy said, "because everybody else is acting like it's real, and I know it's phony. Uncle Jefferson as much as told me he was going to do something like that last night."

"Why *else* would he wear a yellow suit to a revival?"

"Why would he wear a yellow suit, period?"

"All right, get out, Rudy. I have to change into some clothes and go down and see this character." She started to climb out of bed and groaned. "If I ever say I'm going to get a suntan again, tie me up or something, would you?"

"No," Rudy said, "but I'll be glad to gag you."

She threw her pillow at him, and he dodged out of the room.

When Rudy got downstairs, Quintonia was in the kitchen whipping up some scalloped oysters, and Aunt Gussie and Uncle Jefferson were in a corner of the living room, deep in whispered conversation. Rudy was surprised Aunt Gussie was whispering. But then she was never one to, as she put it, air the family's dirty laundry in front of strangers.

But if it were left up to Little Al, Clancy Faith was no longer to be considered a stranger, that was obvious. They were sitting on the sofa together, sipping lemonade and chatting about whether God approved of Babe Ruth.

"God gave him his gift of athletic ability, so of course He approves of his playing baseball," Clancy Faith was saying. "But I know He's unhappy with the Babe's way of life. All that drinking and spending—I'm sure the Lord is very disappointed in that. But it's never too late for Babe or anyone else to repent and begin again. Ah, now who is this vision of beauty?"

Clancy Faith was looking in Rudy's direction, and Rudy was about to answer that he did *not* want to be called a "vision of beauty," when Hildy Helen swept past him in a hurriedly thrown-on polka-dotted dress and offered her hand.

"I'm Hildy Helen Hutchinson," she said. "But please don't

squeeze too hard. I have a sunburn."

"Bless your heart!" Clancy said. "Do you mind if I pray for you?"

Did she mind? Rudy could see her practically drooling as she took in his bulging biceps and his matinee-idol hair. She shook her head and before Rudy knew what was happening, they were all, including Quintonia, gathered around Hildy Helen, placing their hands just above her skin so they wouldn't hurt her, and Clancy Faith was praying for relief from pain and a good night's sleep and the wisdom not to expose her sacred temple of a body to the elements again.

When they were finished, Hildy Helen said, "So how come I'm not healed yet?"

"Hildegarde!" Aunt Gussie said.

But Clancy Faith laughed. "You're a spunky one, aren't you?"

"I guess so," Hildy Helen said. "Not that many people fool me, anyway."

"I'm not trying to fool you at all. You will be relieved of your pain in God's time, and knowing that He's there for you makes it so much easier to bear."

"A lemon ice would make it so much easier to bear, too," she said, looking at Quintonia.

The maid went off muttering to the kitchen, but Rudy caught the smooth look on her face. Clancy Faith sure seemed to have that effect on people—even Hildy Helen.

"Do you really think I'm spunky?" she said.

Yeah, he does, Rudy thought. *And he probably thinks Little Al's charming. Me he hasn't even noticed. That's because I get duller by the minute!*

Quintonia sailed back in with a lemon ice for Hildy Helen and a platter of scalloped oysters for the rest of them, complete with crackers and little pearl onions with fancy toothpicks in them.

"Now, Reverend Faith," she said, "don't you ever tell *anybody* that Quintonia Hutchinson served you something out of a can. These onions—"

"I love these onions. I don't care where they come from," Little Al said.

"Amen," said Clancy Faith. "Would you like me to offer a blessing?"

Almost before the last of the prayer was out of Clancy's mouth, Uncle Jefferson started back in. The tears were now gone, and his impish face was glowing like a filament-filled light bulb.

I gotta give him credit, Rudy thought. *He's good.*

"You have no idea what a victory you've won tonight, Clancy Faith," Uncle Jefferson said. "My life was just like what you were describing in that tent."

"With one correction," Aunt Gussie said. "You have never been a criminal."

"It's criminal to live the way I've been living. I think I've known it for a while—the uneasy feelings that have been creeping in now and then."

Rudy thought about the old-impish looks Uncle Jefferson sometimes got, the ones that made it seem as if he were trying too hard. But still—

"I always thought you was fun, Uncle J," Little Al said.

"I've been fun around you. I'm not always that way," Uncle Jefferson said. "Not when I'm swilling bathtub gin and chasing after flappers half my age and squandering my money on ridiculous things."

"I wondered about that suit," Clancy Faith said. His eyes twinkled merrily.

"No offense, Reverend Faithful, sir," Little Al said, "but you should talk."

Clancy Faith grinned down at his frog-green suit. "I wear this to get attention. Once I have it, then I let the Lord take over."

"Well, I no longer need attention," Uncle Jefferson said. "I've already promised Gussie I'm going to sell the suit tomorrow and give the proceeds to the poor people. Heaven knows there are plenty of them in New York."

"Does this mean you're going to stop telling funny stories?" Hildy Helen said.

"There is no need for anyone to stop being who he is just because he's accepted the Lord," Clancy Faith said. "God loves fun people. He created them!"

"But I'm afraid."

Rudy looked quickly at his uncle. His voice was full of tears again, and they were gathering once more in his eyes. Rudy wanted to roll his. *Here we go again*, he told himself.

"What is it that you're afraid of?" Clancy Faith said.

"I'm afraid that this exhilarating feeling that I have is going to slip away. That I'm going to wake up tomorrow and it's all going to seem like a dream that I can't live." Uncle Jefferson dropped to his knees on the straw-woven carpet and clasped his hands together on Clancy Faith's knees. "Will you help me, Reverend? Will you help me make sure this isn't going to go away?"

Rudy knew if he didn't get out of there, he was going to be in more pain than Hildy Helen. The embarrassment was already turning him as red as her sunburn.

"I gotta go get some air," he said and hurried from the living room.

It was true. The house *was* suddenly stifling. It was as if the air were so heavy with embarrassment—and doubt—that he couldn't breathe.

It was getting windy out, and the air was moist with surf spray as he started the short walk toward the bluff. There were a bunch of heavy clouds rolling in on the wind, but it was still clear enough that when he settled himself down, further from the edge than Marjorie had ventured, he could see the light sweeping over the black ocean. The white foamy edges of the waves raced toward the shore and then disappeared into sparkles on the sand, and their rough rhythm made Rudy feel like he could breathe again—and think again.

Hildy Helen's disappointed that maybe Uncle Jefferson won't be any fun anymore. I think he's being too much fun! Doesn't anybody else see that he's faking?

Rudy pulled his shirt tighter around him against the wind and followed the sweeping light with his eyes. *I'm disappointed that he's carrying this so far. Before you know it, he and Clancy Faith will be traveling as a team—one of them pretending to save souls and the other one pretending to be one of them.*

But is Clancy Faith pretending, the way Uncle Jefferson said he would? Or is he real?

Rudy didn't have a chance to go any farther with that before his eyes snagged on something dark out on the water, darker than the ocean itself. When the light passed over it, Rudy felt his eyes grow wide.

Near the shore, tossing on the stormy water, was a large row-boat, manned by two people. They were struggling to get the craft onto the beach, even though their silhouettes showed strong-looking men.

What are they doing out there with this storm brewing? Rudy thought. Then he shook his head and watched. *I really am getting to be like a boring old man!*

As the wind kicked the waves up higher, the two men managed to get the boat onto the shore and drag it across the sand as if they were in a terrific hurry.

I would be, too, if I thought I was about to get shipwrecked, Rudy thought.

But they didn't continue up the beach with the boat. Instead, they threw some kind of cover off the back end of it and started lifting objects that appeared to be heavy from the way their backs were bending as they hoisted. The wind was beginning to stir up sand in thick bursts, but Rudy shaded his eyes and continued to stare. It was hard to make out what they were hauling out of the boat.

Wish I had Aunt Gussie's spyglass, he thought. *It might actually come in handy.*

All he could detect, with the sand blowing around and the light only sweeping over them at intervals, was a box of some kind and what looked like—

Rudy's eyes bugged out. It couldn't be.

The other objects they were pulling from the boat looked like bodies.

✢✢✢

Chapter Ten

*A*nd *stiff* bodies to boot! The way the two men were carrying them, straight up and down, they couldn't possibly be alive.

Rudy's stomach turned over, but somehow he couldn't just run back to the summer house. All he could think to do was get a better look—prove to himself that those *weren't* dead people he was seeing. The question was, how?

The answer came to him in a flash of Marjorie. She had stretched herself out on her stomach at the edge of the cliff so she could get way over the side to see. Rudy took a deep, sandy breath and wriggled his way to the edge.

I hope I don't look as crazy as she did doing this, he thought.

He knew he didn't look as brave. He was moving like a snail, and his heart was pounding so hard, it hurt to have his chest to the ground this way.

She'd been right, though. He could see better from here. Holding his breath in the wind, Rudy watched the shadowy figures carry their burdens into the sand dunes, and then very shortly come out without them. As they pulled their second load out of the boat, Rudy scooted himself a little further out over the edge of the cliff, but he could see the "bodies" only a little bit better. What he did see made him suck in his breath even harder.

They weren't whole bodies.

They seemed to be cut off somewhere around the legs.

Rudy had seen enough. He rolled over onto his back and stared up at the racing clouds with his heart in his throat.

I gotta tell somebody! he thought frantically.

But this was something that would *really* upset Aunt Gussie.

Rudy rolled back over and peered down to the beach again. The men were disappearing into the dunes once more.

If only I could see better, he thought. *'Cause what if I tell somebody and get Aunt Gussie all sick and upset, and then it turns out to be nothing?*

Once again he thought about the spyglass, perched on the mantel in the summer house living room. Aunt Gussie had said it still worked, that she'd been planning for them to look for whales with it or something.

Rudy scrambled up from the bluff and raced toward the house. How he was going to get out with the thing without anybody noticing was another problem, but maybe they'd all moved to the front porch—or better yet, maybe Clancy Faith had gone away by now and everyone else had gone to bed.

No such luck. Clancy Faith was holding forth in the middle of the living room, and everyone was sitting all around him, hanging on his every word. Just on the outside of their circle was the fireplace, and there on the mantel was the spyglass—up to now ignored, but suddenly the only thing Rudy could think about. How on *earth* was he going to get it out of there?

The question was a tough one, but it brought on a feeling Rudy hadn't felt in a while: the challenge of trying to do something without getting caught. It was such a delicious feeling, one he used to have on a daily—no, *hourly*—basis, that he stood in the doorway for a moment and double-checked it.

Is this okay, God? he thought. *I know it's sneaky, but is it wrong? Is it irresponsible? Would it disappoint Dad?*

"Reverend Faith, you are a delight!" Aunt Gussie said just then. Rudy saw that her eyes were bright, and her wrinkly cheeks were pink, and she was shaking her head of gray Marcel waves in laughter.

This has to be right, Rudy told himself. *It's to keep Aunt Gussie looking happy and calm for Dad.*

Rudy took a deep breath and sidled toward the fireplace.

They were all so engrossed in what Clancy Faith was saying, no one appeared to notice Rudy resting his elbow up on the mantel. Rudy pretended to be captured by the conversation, too, leaning his head forward and nodding whenever Aunt Gussie or Uncle Jefferson did.

"This is how I see it," Clancy Faith was saying. "This younger generation, of which you, Jefferson, have managed to remain a part, is the first one to take itself seriously as a separate, distinct group. There isn't anything wrong with that. In fact, it could be a very good thing. But unfortunately, the young have distinguished themselves in all the wrong ways."

"What wrong ways?" Hildy Helen said. Her sun-red face looked a little indignant.

"Take the flappers. Eight or nine years ago they hiked up their hemlines and cut their hair and did a bunch of crazy dances—everything they could to separate themselves from the way their mothers looked and acted. Here we are, at what I see as the end of the flapper era, and all the flappers have done is establish equal rights in things that don't matter!"

"But women can vote now!" Hildy Helen said. "Doesn't that matter?"

"The flappers didn't get women the right to vote. That was done for them before they started going in for short skirts. Women like your Aunt Gussie won voting for women. And do you want to know something else?"

Everybody nodded.

"According to voting records, very few younger women are even bothering to vote. They're too busy showing everyone that they can smoke and drink whenever and wherever they want to."

"Oh," Hildy Helen said.

"Many of them come here to the Cape in the summers, especially the artsy ones," said Clancy Faith. "Bohemians, they call themselves. Did you see that one couple at the revival meeting tonight?"

Rudy had, but he didn't want to call attention to himself.

"People ask me why I want to come to New England to hold a revival when surely no one will come. Cape Cod is far too trendy to have much patience with such an old-fashioned event." Clancy Faith smiled his light-up-the-room smile. "People like that Bohemian couple who thought they were there to take notes on me and put me in some novel are the very people I'm here to minister to."

Uncle Jefferson raised his hand. "Guilty," he said. "I was there to take mental notes. I was going to portray you on stage next chance I got."

As the attention shifted to Uncle Jefferson, Rudy carefully used his elbow to slide the spyglass to the end of the mantel. If he could push it off the end, he could let it drop into his other hand, pulled behind his back, and slip it under his shirt and get out of the room—maybe without their even knowing he'd been there.

Rudy was glad Uncle Jefferson was still entertaining when he talked. As his uncle went into his pre-revival rendition of Clancy Faith, Rudy silently pushed the spyglass off the end of the mantel.

But to his dismay, nothing fell into his hand. He didn't hear anything hit the floor either.

Trying not to look baffled, Rudy chanced a casual glance over his shoulder. Little Al was just coming up from the floor, a charmer grin cocking his lips upward. Rudy had seen that look before. Little Al now had the spyglass somewhere on his person.

Rudy, of course, wanted to bolt from the room with Little Al behind him. But naturally Uncle Jefferson chose that moment to point to Rudy and say, "You can ask Rudolph. I was all prepared to come home and regale the family with a perfect imitation of you, Reverend Faith—with a few minor modifications of my own, of course."

"Is that true, Rudolph?" said the Reverend Faith. He bulleted his eyes at Rudy.

Rudy felt himself going wooden. This wasn't a conversation he wanted to be involved in, especially not right now. Those men could be gone from the beach by now, and he'd never know what they were carrying.

"I don't know," he said. "But are there any more oysters? Little Al stole mine off my plate."

"Did not!" Al said, grinning.

"You boys are 'bout to eat us outta house and home," Quintonia said. She sighed in exaggerated fashion and headed for the kitchen.

Rudy followed with an ultra-casual swagger. He could feel Little Al doing the same thing behind him. He just hoped Al still had the spyglass.

"While you're fixing more oysters," Rudy said on his way to the back door, "we're gonna go outside for a minute—"

"You are going nowhere of the kind," Quintonia said. "Not with that storm simmering up to a boil out there."

"But I *have* to go outside!"

That came from Hildy Helen, who was standing in the doorway, fanning her face with the front of her dress.

"Put your dress down, girl!" Quintonia said. "You're worse than a flapper!"

"This sunburn is making me so hot!" Hildy wailed. "Can't I just go outside for a couple of minutes until I get cooled off?"

"She looks like she's gonna faint," Little Al said. "Swell!

Reverend Faithful could revive her."

"We'll go outside with her, Quintonia," Rudy said quickly.

"All right," Quintonia said. "But don't come cryin' to me if you get blown away. And the minute it starts to rain, you bring her back in, do you hear me?"

"I promise," Rudy said, and then all three children darted out the back door into the gathering storm.

Rudy bolted for the bluff with Hildy Helen and Little Al right behind him.

"What's goin' on, Rudolpho?" Little Al said.

"I know something's up," Hildy Helen said. "I haven't seen that look on your face in a long time, Rudy."

But Rudy knew the look was gone from his face by this time. He knew all he looked now was scared half to death. Almost shouting over the storm, Rudy filled them in. Little Al's inevitable whistle when he was finished was lost on the wind.

"You do have the spyglass, right?" Rudy said when they reached the bluff.

"Yeah," Little Al said. "But there ain't nothin' to see down there."

Rudy's heart sank when he looked over the cliff and saw that Little Al was right. The beach was empty of everything but blowing sand and waves that seemed to be running in fear from the storm that any minute now was going to break loose.

"Are you sure you saw people down there?" Hildy Helen said.

"I'm not making it up!" Rudy said.

"Don't start squawkin' at each other," Little Al said. "Why don't we go down in the dunes and see if they left them bodies or whatever they were down there."

"Why would they leave them out here?" Rudy said.

"Somebody left a treasure chest, didn't they?"

"What treasure chest?" Hildy Helen said.

"We found one this morning," Rudy said.

"And you didn't tell me?"

"You were on your deathbed, Dollface," Little Al said. "Come on, Rudolpho, whattaya say? Let's go down."

Rudy hesitated. Was this the responsible way to do this?

But who else was going to do it? They sure didn't want Aunt Gussie to know. And Uncle Jefferson and Clancy Faith were too involved in their performance. And Quintonia had nearly had a stroke herself when she'd found the "Sasquatch" footprints.

"All right," Rudy said. "Let's go before it starts raining."

"A little rain never hurt nobody," Little Al said.

"Yeah, but I promised Quintonia—"

The words were hardly out of his mouth before the first drops started to fall. They were big ones, and they stung like bullets of water as the wind smashed them against Rudy's skin.

"We gotta go back to the house," he shouted to Al and Hildy.

"You're such an old fuddy-duddy!" Hildy Helen shouted back.

But he could see that the rain was stinging her sunburn. Her face contorted more the harder it rained.

"Come on, Dollface," Little Al said. "This ain't lookin' good."

They turned toward the house, just as the sky lit up with a startling glare.

"Lightning!" Hildy Helen squealed.

Now who's a fuddy-duddy? Rudy thought.

He bent his head against the rainy wind and started off with his brother and sister behind him. The sky sizzled again, and there was a roar out over the ocean. Rudy glanced back, just as Little Al was doing, and he nearly choked on a mouthful of rain.

The lightning brought two figures into full view as they hurried out of the dunes below. Their faces were clear in the instant the sky was ablaze.

It was the Kelly brothers.

⚓–⚓–⚓

Chapter Eleven

R udy didn't stop. The storm had turned into a tempest, and he could only run on with his heart nearly choking him. The rain was roaring, and lightning was coming in flash after flash, and after it heavy rolls of thunder that seemed to crack open the sky and let out even more rain. But it was the violent wind that took the breath out of Rudy, and all thoughts of the Kelly brothers out of his head.

Behind him, Hildy Helen screamed. When Rudy turned around a gust lifted her right off the ground and then flung her down again. Little Al squatted down to help her, but it looked as if he couldn't get up either.

Rudy put his head down and forced himself to move back to them. By the time he got there he could barely see his hand in front of him. They were already in water over their soles, and it rolled in waves on the ground just like the ocean. Hildy Helen reached up and grabbed onto Rudy's hand, and he put his other hand on Little Al's shoulder. Even at that, Rudy felt like they were all going to go over like a stack of dominoes. He looked around in a panic.

"There's the fence!" he shouted. "Just a couple steps and we can get to it! Grab onto it and hold on!"

He thought Little Al yelled something about that fence being too flimsy, but an angry clap of thunder drowned him out. Rudy started for it, and Hildy Helen clung to his now soaked shirt. Little Al dropped to his hands and knees and crawled through the rising puddles. He got a good arm-lock onto the fence and reached out for Hildy Helen to grab his hand. Rudy got to the fence and curled his arms around it just as the biggest gale yet swept over them, peppering them harshly with a torrent of rain that shook Rudy to the core. They all squeezed their hands around the fence, but it swayed sickeningly with the wind.

Al was right! This'll never hold us!

Rudy was having visions of all three of them being hurled out to sea on the fence and being thrown around by an ocean that was no longer a set of rhythmic waves, but a churning cauldron of chaos. When one of the fence posts ripped up out of the ground, the vision became all too real. Hildy Helen screamed, and Rudy howled right along with her.

And then another voice joined theirs, and with it a body, slanted into the wind as it approached from the direction of the house.

"Grab onto me!" the voice shouted. Even in the midst of the storm, it sounded like a wide-open door.

Hildy Helen threw herself at Clancy Faith, and he picked her up and heaved her over his massive shoulder.

"Alonzo, grab one leg! Rudolph, you get the other one!"

Rudy didn't even hesitate to do what he was told. Clancy Faith's leg felt like a log, sturdy and strong enough to get Rudy all the way across the yard.

The storm swirled around them as the preacher made his way to the house like a man ball-and-chained at his ankles and carrying an 80-pound sack of flour on his shoulder. When the back door opened and Quintonia helped to haul them in, Clancy Faith didn't collapse on the floor. In fact, he was barely breathing hard as he slid Hildy Helen gently onto a chair.

Rudy let go of his leg and straightened up to thank him, but a towel came down over his head and Quintonia barked, "Get those wet shoes off, boy, before you catch your death of pneumonia."

"What on earth were you doing out there?" Aunt Gussie said.

Rudy whipped the towel off his head and shot Hildy Helen and Little Al a warning look. Hildy Helen pursed her lips together. Of course, she hadn't seen what Rudy had seen in that lightning flash. If she had, she would probably be blubbering the whole story at this very moment.

"It's my fault, Miss Gussie," Quintonia said, going after Little Al's head with a second towel. "I should never have let them out that door."

"I needed some air," Hildy Helen piped up.

"Well, you certainly got some," Uncle Jefferson said. Rudy looked at him and for the first time noticed that his uncle's face was gray. So was Aunt Gussie's. In fact, she sank into the chair beside Hildy Helen and breathed hard.

"Are you all right, Aunt Gussie?" Rudy said.

"I'm perfectly fine," she said, "now that you children have had sense enough to come in out of the rain."

"Reverend Faith was our hero!" Hildy Helen said.

"He's the one you oughta be fussing over, Quintonia," Rudy said. He pulled away from her oncoming attack with another towel.

"And fuss over him we shall," Aunt Gussie said. "Reverend Faith, you cannot possibly drive back to Provincetown in this storm."

"Not in that rattletrap you drive," Uncle Jefferson said, eyes twinkling. "Although I suppose now I should consider selling my roadster, too—"

"Please do us the honor of staying here tonight," Aunt Gussie said. "You can have the boys' room. You boys can bunk with Hildy Helen for a night."

"And I have the perfect pair of silk pajamas for you," Uncle Jefferson said. "In fact, you can have them. I'm going to simplify the way I live."

"You don't have to start dressing in horsehair shirts, Jefferson!" Clancy Faith said, laughing.

"Whatever it takes, Clancy. Whatever it takes."

So now they're "Clancy" and "Jefferson," Rudy thought. *I'm telling you, they're going to end up being a team.*

Or are they? Uncle Jefferson's talking about selling his precious car. Clancy Faith practically took his life in his hands to come out and rescue us.

Rudy couldn't figure it out, and he didn't have time to try right now. They had to clear out of their room and make pallets on the floor in Hildy Helen's. They were all dry and ready to climb into them when Aunt Gussie called for them to come downstairs again.

There was a fire going in the fireplace, and Clancy Faith's clothes were hung in front of it to dry. He was wearing a pair of turquoise silk pajamas with the initials JH monogrammed on the front in gold thread. With his muscular build, he was bulging out of them, but he was grinning as if he were wearing a tailor-made suit.

"Come join us, children," Aunt Gussie said. "Reverend Faith is going to bless us with a benediction before we go to bed."

Rudy wanted to groan. More dramatics. He glanced at Hildy Helen, ready to exchange eye rolls, but she was rocking up and down on her toes and watching the preacher as if she were expecting him to perform a miracle right there.

He "performed," all right, as far as Rudy was concerned. When they were standing quietly in a circle, Clancy Faith opened his door of a voice and began to pray.

"Father, this night has been one for the books, hasn't it? How can we thank You for the blessings, the abundant blessings, that You have bestowed on us this evening?"

He went on to thank God for the success of the revival meeting. Rudy hadn't thought of it as much of a success with only three people coming forward, one of them being the questionable Uncle Jefferson. But Clancy Faith thanked God for it anyway, with a voice so warm Rudy could almost feel it on his skin.

Then he thanked God for Jefferson's conversion and for His presence in their discussions here and for giving him, Clancy, the strength to help bring the children in out of the storm. He made Hildy Helen and Rudy and Little Al sound as if they were handpicked by God for special protection.

"Thank You for the honor of bringing them to safety," Clancy said. "They are far too important to You for us to let them be lost."

"Somebody ought to say 'Amen!'" Uncle Jefferson said. Beside Rudy, he squeezed his hand. It made Rudy feel suddenly sad. He was crazy about funny Uncle Jefferson, and his uncle was obviously pretty fond of *him*, too. Too bad Rudy had to find out he was just a phony.

"Somebody *ought* to say 'Amen!'" Clancy Faith said.

"Amen!" Quintonia said. She stomped her foot and sent her hands up over her head. "Tell it, Preacher!"

"Quintonia has had few opportunities to hear you pray, Reverend Faith," Aunt Gussie said. "Continue, if you like."

The magnificent smile spread over the Reverend Clancy Faith's face. "There is nothing in this world I would rather do."

Then the Reverend turned into what Little Al might have called "a dead ringer" for the storm outside.

He started like a first low roll of thunder, and then his eyes flashed a little as if they were flickers of far-away lightning. Before long, the heavens opened, and he let loose with lightning that left no shadows in the room, thunder that set every heart trembling, and a torrent of rain-words that soaked them through their skin.

When he stopped, there was a calm, as if everything had been washed clean and blown back into its rightful place.

Rudy was surprised at that vision in his head. For a few minutes there, he had been almost convinced that Clancy Faith was real. He certainly made Jesus seem close.

Nah, Rudy told himself firmly. *It's more like going to the movies, watching him.*

It was the same way with Uncle Jefferson. He had tears in his eyes again, and Rudy really wished he wouldn't use that particular acting technique.

Quintonia, on the other hand, seemed completely swept away by Clancy Faith.

"Amen, brother!" she cried.

Sadness descended over Rudy like thick fog. *Even if I did believe it was all real*, he thought, *I don't feel anything. I love Jesus, too, but it doesn't make me want to dance around in the middle of the living room.*

Rudy could feel his face going red, and he looked around for someplace to rest his eyes or a way to hold his arms. He really wished this would be over so he could go to bed.

After what seemed like hours—Rudy even checked outside to make sure the sun wasn't already coming up—everyone finally wound down and headed for bed. Rudy was about to worm into his pallet on Hildy Helen's floor for the second time that night when Hildy Helen climbed into her bed and sat there as if she planned to hold court for the rest of the night.

"Rudy," she said, "I want to talk about Marjorie."

Rudy groaned. "She's an oddball. Go to sleep."

"That's funny," Hildy Helen said. "That's not what she said about you. She talked about two things the whole time I was up on the roof with her."

"You was up on the roof with her?" Little Al said.

"Her father—she's *crazy* for him—and you, Rudy."

"Me?" Rudy said. "You're lyin', Hildy Helen!"

"I am not either. She said you were nice and not stupid like most boys."

"Ooh, she's sweet on you, Rudolpho!" Little Al said.

"She is not!" Rudy cried. "Hildy Helen's making this whole thing up!"

"Since when am I a liar, Rudy Hutchinson?" Hildy Helen said, bob tossed back indignantly. "I was sitting out on the roof trying to get cool after you all left and she was on her roof, too, and she came over and before we could even tell each other our names, she was going on about how swell you were. Not that I believed a word, mind you."

She grinned at Rudy, but he only glared at her. If he'd thought he was embarrassed downstairs, he hadn't felt anything. Even his toes were burning red.

"So, Rudolpho," Little Al said. His black eyes were sparking. "Are you gonna ask her out for an ice cream or somethin'?"

"No, I am not!"

"She said you were very mature."

"I don't care what she said! She's blooey. Besides, I don't even like girls."

"Well, thank you very much," Hildy Helen said. She wrinkled her nose at him.

"You keep sayin' this Marjorie doll is blooey," Little Al said, "but I ain't seen it. She seems like a normal dame to me. It's her old lady that's blooey, is what I say."

"Can we change the subject?" Rudy said miserably.

"I like *this* subject!" Hildy Helen said.

"Whadda ya wanna talk about, Rudolpho?"

Anything but this, Rudy thought. And then he blurted out, "We can talk about those two guys I saw when that last big bolt of lightning struck and I turned around."

"What two guys?" Hildy Helen said, Marjorie apparently

forgotten already.

"The Kelly brothers."

"Yeah," Little Al said. "I thought I seen 'em, too."

"*Who* are the Kelly brothers?" Hildy Helen said.

"The guys who took our treasure chest."

"They *took* your treasure chest?"

"You sure it was them, Rudolpho?"

"Yeah."

"Would somebody *please* tell me what's going on?"

By this time, Hildy Helen was up on her knees on the bed, fists doubled and face almost purple. She got a little irritable when she was left out of things. Rudy filled her in quickly, or at least as quickly as he could with her interrupting every seven seconds with another question.

When she was finally satisfied, at least for the moment, Rudy said, "Now, we can't be telling Aunt Gussie about any of this."

"But I thought you were Mr. Honesty now," Hildy Helen said. "Not that that's bad, of course. But I thought you'd run to Aunt Gussie right away."

"She's not supposed to get upset," Rudy said.

Little Al leaned back on his pallet, arms behind his head. "Time was you'da done just about anything to see Miss Gustavio get all riled up. You was the expert at it, is what I say."

"Well, it isn't like that anymore," Rudy said. He sighed and flopped down on his pallet. "We should just go to sleep."

"Nothin' doin'!" Little Al said. He was sitting up again. "We gotta figure out how we're gonna get our booty from them Kelly brothers."

"They said they'd call," Hildy Helen said.

"Huh! They're a coupla crooks is what they are! They got more chests. Now they got bodies, for cryin' out loud! They ain't gonna bother callin' us. That booty's long gone by now."

"So you call them," Hildy Helen said. "You have their number."

"We have to just forget it," Rudy said.

Little Al crawled across his pallet to Rudy's. "Now who's blooey, Rudolpho? That's our stuff!"

"It isn't our stuff. We just found it. It looks like it's really their stuff."

"If it was their stuff, why didn't they just say so?" Hildy Helen said.

"'Cause they're doin' somethin' underhanded, is what I say." Little Al got right into Rudy's face with his. "You're just gonna leave that alone?"

"*We're* gonna leave it alone," Rudy said. "All of us, 'cause that's what Dad would want us to do."

"Nuh-uh," Hildy Helen said. "Dad would want anything illegal to be uncovered so people could be brought to justice."

She sounded a little like Aunt Gussie's parrot, Picasso, rattling off something they'd heard Dad say a hundred times.

"That's what Dad himself would do," Rudy said. "But he doesn't want us in any trouble."

"So call him."

Rudy shook his head. "That would only upset Aunt Gussie. We just gotta let it go."

"You know something, Rudy?" Hildy Helen said. "I liked you a lot better when you weren't such a flat tire."

She flopped herself down into her bed and turned her back on them. Beside him on his pallet, Little Al whispered, "She don't mean nuttin' by that, Rudolpho. She'll get over it by mornin'."

A moment later, Little Al and Hildy Helen were both doing their sleep-breathing, but Rudy was still wide awake. The storm was over, and he could once again hear the rhythm of the ocean, but it wasn't calming tonight. His mind was too full—and not of lost treasure chests or the Kelly brothers or even stiff half-bodies he wasn't even sure were bodies at all now.

It was Uncle Jefferson he was thinking about.

Jesus, isn't it wrong for someone to pretend to believe in You when he really doesn't?

Rudy didn't even get up and try to draw that prayer. It would just look like all his other drawings anyway. Strangely, he fell asleep wondering if he was as boring to Jesus as he was to himself.

✠ ✠ ✠

Chapter Twelve

*H*ildy Helen's floor was hard, and Rudy couldn't sleep anymore once the sun started filtering through her curtains.
He got up and stumbled downstairs to find Clancy Faith already
up, too. He was sitting on the back porch with a cup and saucer.

"Good morning," Clancy said. The open-door voice was softer
this morning, but it was still as warm and rich as the coffee he was
sipping. It made Rudy wonder again if he might not actually be
real, and not a phony like Uncle Jefferson.

"Something troubling you this morning, Rudolph?"

Rudy looked up quickly. Clancy Faith was studying the frown
which was apparently scrunching up Rudy's face.

"Call me Rudy," Rudy said.

"I wanted to. I was just waiting for an invitation. Now I have
one for you—would you like to join me for a walk on the beach?"

"In our pajamas?" Rudy said.

Clancy Faith chuckled at the turquoise getup he was still in.
"I'm game if you are!"

Rudy gave his baggy, striped drawstring pajama pants a hike
and shrugged. "Sure," he said. Dad, after all, wouldn't want him to

be impolite.

The storm had blown the clouds away, and the sky was a seamless blue. If Rudy had tried to paint it in art class back at the Institute in Chicago, his teacher would have said, "The sky is never all one color, Rudy. Put some shading in." But this blue was constant from horizon to horizon. Maybe this was why people flocked to Cape Cod.

Hildy Helen would say that was a pretty boring reason, Rudy thought. *She's probably right.*

"I think the ocean is prettiest early in the morning," Clancy Faith said when they'd climbed down from the bluff and were at the water's edge. "It's as if the sea were whispering to us."

Rudy looked at him suspiciously. "I thought you'd say that was God whispering to us."

"I think I did," said Clancy Faith. "Every good and perfect thing is from God."

That was tricky, the way you handled that, Rudy thought.

"Look what we're about to see!" Clancy Faith said in an excited whisper. He put a hand on Rudy's arm to stop him and pointed out over the ocean.

A pearl gray tern with its black feather hood was poised just above the water. As they watched, the bird dipped neatly beneath the surface and came up with a silvery fish held crosswise in its bill.

"Good catch!" Clancy Faith called to it.

It answered with a cry, without dropping its breakfast.

"Aunt Gussie wouldn't like that," Rudy said. "She always tells us not to talk with our mouths full."

Clancy Faith chuckled. "A fine person, your Aunt Gussie. She says the same thing about you."

"What? That I talk with my mouth full?"

"No, that you're a fine person. I'd have to say, from my observations, that I agree with her."

Now he's trying to butter me up, Rudy thought.

"Thanks," he muttered.

"You're not delighted to be called a fine person?" Clancy Faith said.

"It's all right, I guess," Rudy said. Clancy Faith had called Hildy Helen "spunky" and Little Al a "charmer." Both of those sounded a lot more interesting than "fine."

But what do I care what he thinks of me? Rudy scolded himself. *He's probably a phony anyway!*

Clancy Faith discovered pockets in the pants of the turquoise pajamas and shoved his hands into them. "Tell me something, Rudy," he said. "How did you feel when your Uncle Jefferson was saved last night?"

"Feel?" Rudy said. His thoughts all woke up and began to frantically rub their eyes inside his head.

"You don't show your emotions like the rest of the Hutchinsons, so I just wondered what was going on in that mind of yours."

Rudy started to say, "Oh, I don't know—" but something Hildy Helen had said twice last night raced through his mind before he could get the words out. *You're Mr. Honesty now*, she'd told him. And the second time she'd added, *Not that that's such a bad thing.*

"You really want to know?" Rudy said.

"I wouldn't have asked if I didn't," Clancy Faith said. "I'm in the truth business, after all."

Rudy took in a breath of fishy sea air. "I don't really think he was saved at all. I think he was just putting on an act, and it makes me mad because I don't think a person should mock the Lord that way. Besides, when my Aunt Gussie finds out, she's gonna be upset and probably have another stroke, and I'm supposed to make sure that doesn't happen."

"I see."

Clancy Faith surveyed the ocean with his bullet eyes for a

moment. "What makes you think your Uncle Jefferson's conversion wasn't real?"

"Because he's an actor. He only went there to make fun of you, and he found a pretty sure way to do it. I didn't think he'd go this far, but then he's Uncle Jefferson. If something's fun, he just keeps doing it."

"What about his tears? Those seemed awfully genuine to me."

Rudy was surprised that Clancy Faith wasn't either laughing at him or scolding him for being disrespectful and doubtful. He was instead looking at Rudy the way one adult looked at another in a serious conversation. It made Rudy stand up straighter, even in his striped pajamas, and measure out his words carefully—and truthfully.

"If he was really, really changing his life for Jesus," Rudy said, "why would he carry on like that? That's what I think is phony—all that emotional stuff."

"Go on."

"I love Jesus. I pray every day. I'm trying to do just what my father tells me to do because of that. But I never cried over it. I never got up and danced and waved my arms all around. I think that's all just a big show. No offense, of course. You asked for the truth."

"No offense taken," Reverend Faith said. "But let me make sure I'm hearing you correctly. You think I'm something of a phony myself, is that right?"

Rudy wasn't sure he could actually say it to the man's face. He swallowed hard, and Clancy Faith nodded.

"You certainly have a right to your opinion, Rudy," he said. "But I would like to give you a piece of important information."

"Sure."

"Experiences like the one your Uncle Jefferson had are very real. Why would God *not* do something spectacular when some-one accepts His Son as Lord? That would make Him a pretty uninteresting God!"

Rudy felt as if he'd just been stung by a jellyfish. He'd never had that kind of experience—not ever. Did that mean he wasn't a real Christian?

"Now, as for me," Clancy Faith went on, "I can understand why people are suspicious of my authenticity. They're always suspicious of God's mysteries because they can't be explained. Do you know about Billy Sunday?"

"I've heard of him," Rudy said. "Uncle Jefferson was hoping that was who was coming here."

"And with good reason! Now, there's a man who puts on a show! He's so flamboyant that naturally many people think he's phony as a $3 bill. But let me tell you a little story about Billy Sunday."

He gave Rudy a questioning look, and Rudy nodded. It couldn't hurt anything.

"There was a fella who was a newspaper reporter, and his assignment was to go out and show Billy Sunday for a fake. So this fella went to a town where Billy Sunday had been preaching, and he just talked to people. Well, the store owners told him that during the meetings and afterward, people came to their stores and paid bills that were so old they had dust on them. The reporter went to another town, and the president of the Chamber of Commerce there told him that if Billy Sunday wanted to come back, he could raise the money in half a day from men who never go to church. The reporter got those kinds of answers everywhere he went. He kept asking, 'But didn't Billy Sunday take up collections and leave here with thousands of dollars?' And one fella in a small town said, 'He left here with $11,000, but a circus comes here and takes out that much in one day and leaves nothing. Billy Sunday left a whole different feeling in this town—a good feeling.'"

Clancy Faith gave Rudy a soft version of his magnificent smile. "That's the whole reason for the religious revival we've had in this decade—to get people's attention back on God," he said. "If we have to, we get out and shout and dance and sing and 'perform', if you will, to get the focus away from those high-brows who say Christianity is bunk, from those people who are worshiping success and money instead of God. Once we get their attention with a flashy suit or some acrobatics, great things happen, and they happen because when Christ is allowed to come in, everything around gets washed clean. Just like your Uncle Jefferson there."

"Where?" Rudy said.

He looked, startled, to where Clancy Faith was pointing. Uncle Jefferson was coming toward them, hands in his pockets, face toward the sand. Rudy felt a deep pang.

How long had Uncle Jefferson been out here? Had he heard Rudy talking about him?

I was just telling the truth, though. Why should that matter?

But when Uncle Jefferson looked up, Rudy was relieved to see that he seemed surprised to see them. And then his face snapped from its faraway look to an impish grin.

"What are you two characters doing out here on the beach at this time of night?" he said.

"Night?" Rudy said.

"Since I don't usually get up before noon, this is night to me! But I think that's all about to change, eh, Clancy?"

"If that's how God leads you," Clancy said.

"I hope He doesn't lead me to give up Quintonia's cooking. She's up there at this very moment making blueberry pancakes—with fresh blueberries."

"God's never led *me* to give them up!" Clancy Faith said. "Take me to them!"

As they turned and headed back toward the summer house, Uncle Jefferson said, "What about the suntan? Am I going to have to give up the suntan?"

Clancy Faith laughed. Rudy shook his head as he followed

them. *You sure aren't very smart, Reverend Faith*, he thought, *if you can't see through that*.

Clancy Faith went back to Provincetown right after breakfast, but since Uncle Jefferson had a few more days before he had to return to New York, he made a vow to go to the revival meetings every night until he left.

More "research," Rudy thought. *Either that, or he is just having too much fun with this game.*

Rudy went to the meetings, too, without the argument Little Al and Hildy Helen sometimes put up. There were four reasons for Rudy.

One, Rudy wanted to be there if and when Uncle Jefferson admitted that the whole thing was a joke.

Two, Rudy had to make sure Aunt Gussie was all right.

Three, he wanted to watch Clancy Faith some more. Some things he'd said on the beach had Rudy wondering if he really *was* a phony.

The fourth reason he didn't like to think about, but it kept popping into his head: maybe if Rudy went enough times and really listened, he, too, would have an "experience." Maybe God would do something spectacular in him, and then he could be sure he was a real Christian.

The second night there were twice as many people in the tent as there had been the first night, and on the third night, a person who didn't get there early could hardly find a place to sit down. The money overflowed from the collection plate, and more and more people were coming forward, crying, while others let out the occasional loud "amen" or moved around in their places when the music played.

"Great things are happening," Clancy Faith said to the Hutchinsons after the third night. Then he looked straight at Rudy and smiled his magnificent smile.

But Rudy couldn't smile back, because so far, none of those

"great things" had happened to him. In fact, it was even getting harder to pray out drawings. He put his pens and paper away and didn't take them out again.

Meanwhile, Aunt Gussie went on with the rest of her plans for their summer. She announced at the breakfast table one morning that today was the day she was going to go antique hunting in Provincetown.

"Who wants to come with me?" she said.

"Not me!" Little Al said. "If you don't mind my sayin' so, Miss Gustavio, I think them antique dealers is a buncha crooks."

"You mean, we don't have to go if we don't want to?" Hildy Helen said loudly.

"Hildegarde, how many times do I have to tell you to keep your voice down?" Aunt Gussie said. "A young lady does not yell indoors as if she were at the horses."

"Sorry," Hildy Helen said, "I just got excited. I would really rather find out if Marjorie can play instead of dragging around looking at a bunch of old—" Rudy poked her. "I think I'd rather be neighborly today. And I haven't seen her since—well, in a while."

Aunt Gussie gave her a dry look. "Rudolph, will you join me? Or do you, too, have an aversion to 'crooks' and old heaven-knows-what?"

"I'll go," Rudy said. He tried not to sound like he'd rather be shot, and he promised himself that Little Al and Hildy Helen would pay him back later.

Although he went to Provincetown every night for the revival meetings, Rudy had never been there in the daytime, and he decided that at least it was more interesting than Wellfleet. Instead of roadside apple stands, there were grocery stores. Instead of makeshift places to pick up greasy fried chicken, there were real restaurants with homemade clam chowder. And there were actually *people* around, tourists and summer folks crowding the old, narrow streets with their shopping bags and their loud chatter. Hildy Helen, Rudy decided, would have fit right in.

He figured out right away how to tell the summer people from the Outer Cape Cod natives. The out-of-towners shrieked and yelled to each other across the street and snarled when cars wouldn't stop to let them jaywalk. The Cape Codders just watched them with humorous eyes, and Rudy heard a couple of them chuckle quietly as if they were highly amused at the ways of the outside world.

The things that delighted Aunt Gussie the most, of course, were the real antique shops. These weren't just old barns with shingle signs on them, full of somebody's old attic junk. These were well-polished shops that made a person want to whisper when he went inside.

Rudy kept his elbows close to his sides in the first shop as he followed Aunt Gussie down an aisle filled on both sides with cut crystal that tinkled softly at their footsteps. It was so dimly lit in there, Rudy had to squint through his glasses to see. He hoped he wouldn't step on anything too valuable.

While a small, slick-haired man wearing thick glasses chatted with Aunt Gussie about the figurehead she was searching for, Rudy prowled further into the shop.

I wonder how much this stuff really is worth, he thought. *Those two guys—those Kelly brothers—they seemed to think they were the richest thing since—*

Rudy stopped dead in the aisle. No sooner had he thought of the Kelly brothers than he found himself standing in front of an antique chest.

It wasn't an old sea chest like the one he and Little Al had found. This one looked more like a blanket chest, and the tag said it was made of teakwood. It also said it was $100.

Rudy gave a low whistle, but his thoughts pattered back to the other night on the beach, when he'd seen the Kelly brothers dragging things out of a boat and into the sand dunes.

I betcha they aren't antique dealers at all, he thought. I don't see anything in here that looks like bodies!

He ran his finger along the chest. The wood was smooth, but he shivered. It made him think of *their* sea chest and of the Kelly brothers running up the beach in the storm after pulling stuff off a boat in the dark.

Suddenly the whole shop was giving him the willies. Rudy edged toward Aunt Gussie, and he was relieved to see her pointing her walking stick in the direction of the front door.

"Now you'll be sure to let me know if you get some in," she was saying.

"Of course, of course, of course," the thick-glasses man said. He waved Aunt Gussie's engraved calling card and then brought it close to his glasses to peer at it.

"Hmm!" Aunt Gussie said to Rudy when they were out the door. "If he does find one, we're going to have to do some bargaining. I've never seen such prices!"

"Yeah, a hundred dollars for a stupid blanket chest."

"I can only imagine what he'd want for a figurehead. Although I don't know what I expect. Prices are soaring everywhere, and no one seems to think a thing of it. Look at this!" She stopped in front of a grocery store and poked her finger at the glass. "Five cents for a loaf of bread! It's scandalous! And the shelves in there are just groaning with goods. You just mark my words, Rudolph. The higher they go, the harder they fall. There's going to be a crash, one we won't recover from. But does anyone listen to me? All I hear when I say that this prosperity is due for a decline, is, 'Why, Gussie, we've scarcely started!' It's something I want to discuss with Reverend Faith."

Rudy noticed the veins bulging in her neck, and he got nervous.

"So what exactly does a figurehead look like?" Rudy said.

"If we're lucky, we'll find one in here," she said, and she steered him into yet another shop, this one even darker and more crammed with musty-smelling pieces of furniture than the other one.

Aunt Gussie headed straight for the beak-nosed man who was coming down the center aisle. This man had a toothy grin and lots of wavy hair, and he looked as if he were going to ask Aunt Gussie to dance, not sell her antiques.

Rudy started to follow his aunt, when his attention snagged on another chest, set on top of a pile of stuff that looked as if it had just come in and hadn't been put on display yet. This one was almost identical to the one he and Al had found. It didn't have a padlock on it, but when Rudy tried to open it, it resisted. Then he saw that it had a keyhole.

Huh. I don't remember one on ours 'cause it had a padlock.

Rudy looked around, but Aunt Gussie and the toothy man were deep in conversation. Rudy shrugged and began to poke at the lock with his index finger. Little Al would have whipped some tool out of his pocket and had the thing unlocked by now.

The shop door bell jangled behind him, and Rudy jumped. His finger slid deeper into the keyhole, and he tried to yank it out before whoever had just come into the shop could see him making a fool of himself.

But his finger wouldn't budge.

Aw, man! he thought. *I'm such a klutz!*

"Why, Rudy!" said the person in the doorway. "I had no idea you were an antique hound!"

Rudy turned his head to see Mr. Sandy Potter smiling at him.

✣ ✤ ✣

Chapter Thirteen

*H*ow are you, son?" Mr. Sandy said.

He stuck out his hand to shake Rudy's, and Rudy had to reach across himself with his left hand to return the handshake. His right pointer finger stayed stuck in the keyhole.

Mr. Sandy's chocolate phosphate eyes twinkled. "You seem to have a bit of a problem there," he said as he squeezed Rudy's hand and let him have it back. He glanced around the shop and smiled his handsome smile. "Perhaps we can get it taken care of without anyone being the wiser, do you think?"

"I hope so," Rudy said. He felt like an idiot, but at least Mr. Sandy wasn't chewing him out or, worse, laughing at him. He was beginning to see why Marjorie was so all-fired crazy about her father.

"Let's just have a look—" Mr. Sandy leaned his tall frame over to examine Rudy's finger and then took hold of it and gave it a firm squeeze. "Take a nice deep breath," he said.

Rudy did, and with an easy pull from Mr. Sandy his finger came right out. And not a moment too soon. From down the aisle, he could hear Aunt Gussie's walking stick thumping the floor, and Mr.

Teeth saying, "I will most certainly call you about those figure-heads, Mrs. Nitz. I would consider it an honor to make a sale to a woman as obviously sophisticated and knowledgeable as yourself."

When Rudy looked up, rubbing his finger behind his back, Aunt Gussie was rolling her eyes at him while Mr. Teeth droned on at her back. Leave it to Aunt Gussie to spot a phony a mile away.

"Now mind you, those figureheads are rare," the man went on, "but I'm just certain that—"

And then his eyes lit on Sandy Potter, and something happened. Mr. Teeth seemed to wilt, from his thick waves to his spotless white spats.

"Uh, hullo, uh, Mr. Potter, sir," he said. "I . . . uh . . . I wasn't expecting you in today."

Mr. Sandy's eyes ran over the pile of new arrivals topped by the trunk and nodded. But that was only for a second. He smiled at once at Aunt Gussie and said, "I don't believe I've had the pleasure. I'm Sanford Potter."

"We're neighbors for the summer," Aunt Gussie said, offering her hand in that classy way she had. "It's nice to know there's a strong man next door, there being so few of us out on Wellfleet."

"And I'm afraid I won't be much good to you most of the time," Mr. Potter said. "I work in Boston and only get out now and then to see to my family and do a little business with Mr. Zork here."

"Perhaps I could call on one of your servants, then, if I have a need," Aunt Gussie said.

"Can't help you there, either, I'm afraid," Mr. Potter said, smiling even more handsomely than before. Rudy noticed that, like Uncle Jefferson, Mr. Sandy was sporting a golden tan. "My wife and daughter are going it on their own this summer, with a cook and a housekeeper, that is," Mr. Potter went on.

What about Louis? Rudy thought, although he had to admit he hadn't seen the white-suited man since the day they'd rescued him.

Aunt Gussie must have been thinking the same thing, because she looked puzzled. "Oh," she said. "That's odd. But, no matter. My mistake."

"We don't need Mr. Sandy's servants anyway, Aunt Gussie," Rudy said hurriedly. "You got me."

"I don't see how you could possibly require anything else," Mr. Sandy said. He gave Rudy's shoulder a squeeze. "Rudy here's a fine specimen of a young man."

As the good-byes were said—and Mr. Sandy got in a wink to Rudy on the sly—Rudy decided he really did like the man. It didn't matter about Louis anyway. That had probably just been somebody playing a prank. The thought of Mr. Sandy's kindness chased even that away.

Rudy didn't consider until later when he and Aunt Gussie were eating ice cream in a parlor across the street that everybody didn't react to Mr. Sandy the way he did. He had seemed to make Mr. Zork pretty nervous. It was almost as if the antique dealer had been putting on an act for Aunt Gussie—well, that was obvious—and he couldn't do it in front of Mr. Potter.

"Penny for your thoughts, Rudolph," Aunt Gussie said. She slipped a spoonful of vanilla ice cream into her mouth and watched him as she let it melt in there.

"I was just thinking what a phony that Mr. Zork guy was," Rudy said. "Mr. Potter sure saw through him, huh?"

"Or Mr. Zork saw through Mr. Potter, I don't know which," Aunt Gussie said. "I won't deny that he was turning on the charm to make a sale. But Mr. Potter certainly made him nervous, didn't he? Interesting."

"Interesting how?" Rudy said.

But Aunt Gussie scraped the bottom of her dish and said, "I find it strange that no one seems to have any figureheads. It's hard to believe they're that scarce."

"What is a figurehead, anyway?" Rudy said.

Aunt Gussie looked surprised. "I haven't shown you a picture, Rudolph?" she said. "Good heavens! Well, it's a wooden figure of a woman placed on the bow of a ship back in your ancestors' time. It was something of a good luck charm, I suppose, though I'm sure Josiah Hutchinson didn't see it that way, good Christian man that he was." She sighed. "I suppose it's just my attempt to save some of what has come before me, just as I'm going to pass on my treasures to you children."

Her face suddenly got a faraway look, and Rudy felt a dull ache somewhere. *She thinks she isn't going to be around for long or something*, Rudy thought. It became more important than ever for him to protect her from everything.

"Come along, Rudolph," she said. "We have more looking to do. And we have to get back in time to get ready for the revival meeting."

But Rudy kept thinking about the incident. He told Little Al about it that afternoon—minus the part about his finger in the keyhole—when Aunt Gussie had finally satisfied herself that there wasn't a ship's figurehead in all of Provincetown and agreed to go back to the summer house.

He and Al and Hildy Helen were digging clams on the beach when Rudy brought it up. Little Al leaned on his shovel and gave it serious thought, his dark eyebrows knitted together.

"We're never gonna get our chest back, Rudolpho," he said. "I'm sure of it, now that we're pretty sure them Kelly brothers is up to no good. I gotta confession to make."

"What?" Rudy said.

"I tried callin' that number on the card."

"Al, I thought I said we were gonna leave it alone!"

"You *did* leave it alone. And anyway, some doll on the other end said they was travelin' in Europe collectin' stuff for their next show."

"Good," Rudy said. "It gave me the creeps seeing them out

here that night. I betcha Mr. Sandy wouldn't like it if he knew they were doing whatever it is right behind his house."

"I don't know," Little Al said. "I kinda wish they'd come back, if ya know what I mean. It would liven things up around here. I had the boringest day. I searched the whole sand dunes *again*, and I didn't find nothin'. You sure you saw them hauling stuff up in boats, Rudolpho?"

"You saw it, too!" Rudy said.

Hildy Helen finally looked up from her clam shovel. "We only saw the Kelly brothers," she said. "We didn't see anybody dragging bodies up like you think you did."

"I did!" Rudy said.

"Oh, I believe you," Hildy Helen said. She waved him off with her shovel. "I'm with Little Al. I'm just wishing something exciting would happen. Now that my sunburn's better and I can move around again, I want to *do* something."

"I thought you were gonna find Marjorie," Rudy said.

"I couldn't. She wasn't home. At least, that was what her mother said. I wonder if they sent her back to Boston or something."

"Nope," Little Al said. "Here she comes now."

They all looked up at the bluff, and sure enough, there was Marjorie Potter making her way down at a much faster pace than Rudy ever took it. *She makes me look like a little old lady*, he thought.

That wasn't all he thought. In fact, he ignored a couple of good clam bubbles to poke his shovel uncomfortably in the sand. It didn't matter what Hildy Helen said about the girl being so nice and thinking he was her friend. The last time he'd talked to her, she'd all but shoved him off the bluff. He didn't think having her join them for a clam dig was all that good an idea.

But join them she did, and Hildy Helen ran and hugged her like they were old pals.

"Why do girls have to do that stuff?" Rudy whispered to Little Al.

"You got me, Rudolph," Little Al hissed back. "I'm tellin' ya, the dolls get more confusing as we get older."

Marjorie Potter was *definitely* confusing. When Hildy Helen finally turned her loose, she looked at the boys with a smile that out-dazzled her father's and said, "Hello, Rudy, Little Al. I'm glad I got to see you again!"

"You are?" Little Al said.

"Of course she is," Hildy Helen said. "Rudy, why are you standing there with your mouth wide open?" She rolled her eyes and turned to Marjorie. "Don't pay any attention to them. Boys can be so rude at this age."

"That's all right. My mother says men are born that way and women have to civilize them. I don't think my daddy was ever uncivilized, though. Oh!" She nodded her blonde head toward their pail, which contained a pitiful three small clams. "I see you're scratching!"

"Never in public," Little Al said. "Miss Gustavio says it ain't polite."

Marjorie made a husky sound in her throat. "Not that kind of scratching. I'm talking about digging your own clams. I love to do it, but my mother says a girl of my class shouldn't. So we buy ours at the fish market—except when my daddy is here, and when he has time, he scratches with me."

Rudy watched Marjorie light up, as if she had her face near a birthday cake full of candles. She pointed it right at him then and said, "Can I scratch with you, Rudy?"

Little Al gave a grunt, and Rudy felt his face going red, but he shrugged and said, "Uh, sure, I guess so."

She started to take the little shovel Quintonia had given him, but she cocked her bob to the side. "Um, you know, you really can get them better with a clam rake. Personally, though, Daddy and I prefer the hand method anyway." She dropped to her knees. "Come on, I can show you."

Hildy Helen got right down there with her. Little Al looked at Rudy, who shrugged for the millionth time and joined her.

"Daddy says most of the clams out here are quahogs. They're bigger and have heavier shells. So if you watch for the two little spout holes you can see where they are and then you just scoop them out of the mud. Like this!"

She stuck a pink hand that looked as if it had never been within a hundred feet of wet sand into the muck and came up with a clam and a grin. "See?" she said. "It's easy! Try it!"

Hildy Helen did, and so did Little Al, and they both produced four clams within the next three minutes. Hildy Helen squealed the entire time, and Little Al talked to them as if they were gangsters he'd just handcuffed and was throwing into a paddy wagon. Rudy managed to trap one, and he took his time about getting it into the pail.

"We won't need as many of these as the other kind," Marjorie said to him when he reluctantly sank to his knees again. "These are only chowder clams—oh, and some people stuff and bake them. Yum!" She lowered her voice. "So don't worry if you can't get a whole lot of them." Then she winked, and for a second Rudy was sure he was looking at Sandy Potter, not his daughter.

As Hildy Helen and Little Al competed to see who could contribute the most to the pail, Rudy breathed a little easier and took the time to examine the ones he did manage to scoop up. Some were thick-shelled and covered most of the palm of his hand. But one was small and smoke-blue and had a shell that was nearly transparent.

"You've found a steamer, Rudy!" Marjorie said. "They're a lot sweeter."

"Hey, Rudolpho! Them clams ain't the only thing sweet around here!" Little Al called out.

Bless him. It gave Rudy an excuse to haul himself up from his hands and knees, grab Little Al around the neck, and drag him into the surf. They wrestled in the water while the girls squealed. Little Al won the match, of course, but at least it got the red out of Rudy's face.

By sunset, when it was time to get ready to go to the revival meeting, they had plenty of clams for chowder and had even had time for building a giant sand city—Marjorie's idea.

As they headed reluctantly toward the house with Quintonia shrieking for them, Hildy Helen said, "Marjorie, come find us first thing in the morning down here on the beach."

"She can't," Rudy said. "Her mother won't let her come out until afternoon."

"I can now!" Marjorie said, china face beaming. "My daddy's here, and he lets me."

"Yeah, her daddy lets her," Hildy Helen said to Rudy with a scowl.

When Marjorie had skipped off to her house, still chattering away, Hildy Helen's frown got deeper, and she punctuated it by punching her hands onto her hips.

"Why did you say that about her not being able to come out in the morning, Rudy?" she said. "You made it sound like you didn't want her to come."

"I'm not sure I do," Rudy said. He pretended to examine the contents of the clam pail.

"Why? 'Cause she's sweet on ya?" Little Al said.

"She is not! And that's not why!"

"Then what is it?" Hildy Helen said.

Rudy shrugged.

"Rudolph Hutchinson," Hildy Helen said, "if you do that with your shoulders one more time, I'm going to scream."

"You're already screaming," Rudy said.

"I don't understand you!"

"And I don't understand *her*!" Rudy said. "I think she's being a phony right now, and sooner or later her true self is gonna come out again."

"You're talkin' about the self you saw the first night when she dragged ya out on the bluff?" Little Al said.

"She didn't 'drag' me."

"No, I bet she didn't," Hildy Helen said. "And I bet she wasn't as mean and crazy as you said she was, Rudy. How could she be? She's so . . . nice . . . and fun . . . and wonderful!"

Rudy stared at his sister. She sounded for all the world like she was going to cry any minute.

"Are you bawlin'?" he said.

"I might be! Finally we get another girl to play with us so I don't always have to do all this boy stuff, and you try to run her off!"

"But she's nuts," Rudy said.

"She sure didn't seem nuts to me, Rudolpho," said Little Al. "Maybe you just thought she was because it was night or somethin'. Maybe ya just got spooked."

"I didn't get spooked," Rudy said stubbornly. "She acted like a crazy person."

"Maybe she did," Hildy Helen said tearfully, "but she's not acting that way now, and I want her around. Don't you, Al?"

Little Al squinted toward the back porch they were approaching as if he hoped gangsters would appear and he'd have to take them on rather than answer that question.

"All right, let her come around," Rudy said. "But you'll see what I'm talking about. She's gonna show her true self sooner or later. Everybody does."

"They do?" Little Al said. "How do you know?"

"I don't know," Rudy said. And that was true. He wasn't sure why he'd even said it. But now that it was out of his mouth, he knew he was right. It made going to the revival that night as important as ever—and as nerve-wracking.

But even though there were more people at the meeting that

night—in fact, some people had to stand up in the back—and more and more people came forward to be saved, Uncle Jefferson kept up his act, and, of course, so did Clancy Faith.

The preacher practically acted out the story of the Samaritan who was better than all the highfalutin bigwigs who passed the injured man by. He drew a vivid picture with his words of the widow with a couple of pennies for the mite box being better than the rich people who bragged about how much they put in the collection plate. It all made sense to Rudy. *It should*, he thought. *It's all about not being phony!*

He dug into his pocket and gave his penny-candy money when the "love offering" basket came along, already heaped with wads of money. But when it came time for the shouting and the crying and the dancing and the amening, Rudy felt nothing at all. Just like all the other nights, he couldn't even say "amen" and mean it.

Am I really a Christian then? he kept thinking.

The lack of an answer was slowly putting him in a cloudy mood.

It didn't help that the next morning, the minute they'd finished breakfast and headed for the beach, Marjorie was already there, clam rakes in hand.

"Later today we can use these," she said when they joined her. "Scratching is better late in the day. But for now, we can keep building our sand city. See, the tide didn't even touch it! I told you if we built it there, it would stay."

She went right on planning the rest of their day, and Hildy Helen followed cheerfully. Rudy got Little Al aside as soon as he could.

"I told you she was bossy," he said.

"Yeah," Little Al said. "But ya gotta admit, Rudolpho, she's kinda fun."

At lunch that day, Hildy Helen declared that the summer had finally livened up and maybe it wasn't going to be so bad staying here for another month or so after all.

It took several weeks for Rudy to decide that *maybe*, but only maybe, Hildy Helen was right about that. At first, all he could think about was that Marjorie was making him look like a case for the loony bin by acting so normal when he'd told his brother and sister she was a nut case. He kept hoping she would do something at least a little bit crazy.

But as Marjorie joined them every day, she just seemed to make things better. She took tired-out games like hide-and-seek and tag and turned them into new ones they'd never tried before. When it rained, she dragged huge canvas covers over from her house, and they made waterproof forts in the Hutchinsons' backyard. Although when they used the spyglass to look for whales they didn't find any, Marjorie made it all right by providing bags of penny candy her father had brought from Boston as a consolation. She had been right; the licorice *was* so juicy it ran out of your mouth.

As time went by and the four children became like a well-matched set of auto wheels, Rudy thought less and less about how Marjorie was that first night he'd met her—especially when Mr. Sandy piled all of them into his velvet-seated Peerless to take them to Provincetown for malts or gave them all Chiclets just for being good-looking children. Marjorie's pink face glowed, and Rudy wondered if he had really heard her say rude things to him ever.

Any suspicions Little Al had about her were washed away the day they were all drawing big pictures in the wet sand with sticks. Little Al saw what Marjorie was drawing first.

"Hey, Marge," he said. "I seen that before."

Marjorie stuck her stick into the sand and nodded without looking at any of them. "I know," she said.

Hildy Helen abandoned her own drawing of a lopsided flapper girl and stared. "It looks just like the Sasquatch footprints we found by the pump house that day."

"It is them," Marjorie said. She still didn't look up, and her voice wasn't its usual chirping-cheerful.

"I knew it!" Little Al said. "Didn't I tell ya, Rudolpho? I said she done it—"

"Al!" Hildy Helen said. "That's rude! You aren't even giving her a chance to explain."

"I was trying to scare you all away," Marjorie said.

"Why?" Hildy Helen said. "You said you liked Rudy the first night you met him."

Rudy tried not to groan out loud.

"I did," Marjorie said. "But my mother said I wasn't going to be allowed to play with him, or any of you, and I thought I couldn't stand to be next door and watch you out doing fun things all the time and not be able to do them with you, so I tried to scare you away, because I heard you talking about Sasquatch that day, and I thought you would just pack up and leave." She looked up and blinked her green eyes at Rudy. "But you didn't."

"I don't understand," Hildy Helen said.

"But then Daddy came here, and you all came over, and afterwards he told my mother she was being silly and that out here on the Outer Cape it was fine for me to go out and play with other children—she didn't need to worry about me here. So here I am, and I'm so sorry I tried to scare you."

"Oh," Hildy Helen said. "But why is she so afraid something's going to happen to you?"

But Little Al cut her off. "Ya know," he said to Marjorie, "I like a doll that's honest. Ya come clean with us just now, and I like that. You're a regular guy, Marge."

So there was only Rudy left with doubts about Marjorie then—until the day Marjorie finally showed her crazy side again.

They were all sitting around after several hours of playing Parcheesi on a cloudy afternoon, and Little Al said, "These are the kinda times I used to sneak away someplace and smoke myself a Lucky Strike."

"Don't even bring that up," Hildy Helen said, poking her brother. "Rudy'll have a fit."

"I never smoked a cigarette," Marjorie said. "Only a cigar."

Hildy Helen sat straight up. "Nuh-uh! You never smoked a cigar!"

"Yes, I did. I used to do it all the time when my daddy went away and I couldn't stand being shut up in the house all the time. I wanted to do something that would make my mother really mad, only I didn't want her to find out. So I'd go to the pump house and smoke a cigar. I don't have to do it now, though, because Daddy has been here all these weeks—"

"I'm havin' a hard time thinkin' a you pickin' up old stogies and lightin' 'em up," Little Al said.

"I didn't smoke old ones!" Marjorie said, looking a little insulted. "I got good ones out of my daddy's desk and some matches and hid them out there."

"I just don't believe you!" Hildy Helen said.

Rudy did. This was an awful lot like a conversation he and Marjorie had had before, and it was making his stomach queasy. He was about to change the subject when Marjorie scrambled up and put her hands on her hips. Rudy groaned. She was spending too much time with Hildy Helen. She was starting to act just like her.

"I won't be called a liar, Hildy Helen Hutchinson!" Marjorie said. "Come on over to our pump house, and I'll show you!"

"How will we know it's your stuff?" Hildy said. "It could be Louis's—"

"I don't *know* any Louis!" Marjorie said. "And I *will* prove it to you. I'll smoke a cigar."

Little Al was grinning. "Right there in front of us?" he said.

"I don't know—" Rudy said.

But it was too late. Marjorie had already upset the Parcheesi board getting out of the room, and Hildy Helen was hot on her trail.

"I like a doll like her," Little Al said, and he followed at a dead run.

Rudy had no choice but to follow. By the time he got there, Marjorie had undone a bolt and flung open the door, but everybody was still standing there staring.

"What are you looking at?" Rudy said. "Is it full of cigars?"

But when he finally got a glimpse of the inside of the pump house, he wished it *was* cigars he was seeing. It was a sea trunk, just like the one Rudy and Al had found on the beach. The one the Kelly brothers had taken away.

"Hey!" Little Al said before Rudy could stop him. "That's—"

"A sea trunk!" Rudy said.

Hildy Helen wriggled in to get a closer look. "Is it like the one—"

"I saw with Aunt Gussie in an antique shop? Yes! Mr. Sandy must've bought it the day I was in there. I ran into him that day. Did I tell you?"

Hildy Helen glared at him. "Can a person finish a sentence, Rudy?" she said.

By that time, Marjorie, who had temporarily lost her tongue, piped back into the conversation. "My daddy collects antiques all the time. Our house in Boston is crammed with them. This one must be broken. Yes, you see that. It's all scratched up. He keeps the broken stuff out here. Yeah, that's right. Hey, anybody want to smoke a cigar *with* me?"

It only took Little Al a second to shift gears and say, "And how!"

"Sure," Hildy Helen said. "I'll try it!"

"Says who?" Rudy said.

Three pairs of eyes flicked to him.

"Are you blooey?" he said. "Do you know how much trouble we'd get into if we got caught? Nuh-uh, nothing doing. Come on. Let's go . . . play giant Parcheesi in the sand. We'll make driftwood our playing pieces—"

"I like that!" Marjorie said. "Only we have to find different colors. I want white. I love white! What's your favorite color, Hildy Helen?"

As Hildy Helen explained, rather irritably, that it was red but there was certainly no red driftwood on the beach, they all left the pump house, and Rudy bolted it behind them.

He had an uneasy feeling, and thoughts of the Kelly brothers and the trunk and that night in the storm all relocated themselves to the front of his brain again. And for some reason, from then on, he wanted to protect Marjorie Potter.

✢ ✢ ✢

Chapter Fourteen

*W*hile the summer days of 1929 passed in a colorful stream of clams and sand cities and crab-cake picnics on the beach, the evenings happened like vivid bursts that grew bigger and more spectacular every night.

Clancy Faith's suits got brighter. The music got more lively—more "joyful," he always said. The Bible stories grew more dramatic, until Clancy Faith had everybody in tears as Jesus died on the cross.

Everybody but Rudy was so wrapped up in Clancy's journey of faith, they didn't seem to notice that Rudy didn't feel the same way. They barely noticed that Uncle Jefferson stayed on past his week of vacation, and then another week, and still another. Once Rudy heard Aunt Gussie ask him about it, and he said, "Baby Sister, you worry too much! You don't think I've taken care of it?"

"What? Do you have an understudy or something?" Aunt Gussie said.

"Something like that, yes."

"Aren't you afraid you'll lose your part?"

"Clancy has taught me, 'Be not afraid.' I'm living what I know,

Baby Sister. I'm living what I know."

That almost convinced Rudy that maybe Uncle Jefferson was not faking his new walk with the Lord after all. But once again, Rudy was disappointed.

It happened toward the beginning of the last week of the Reverend Clancy's stay. He came home with the Hutchinsons after the meeting for a late supper, as he often did, and they were all eating scalloped oysters around the kitchen table, when suddenly Uncle Jefferson put his fork down and started to cry. It was getting to be a common sight to see him break out bawling with joy during a revival meeting, and it still embarrassed Rudy nearly to tears. But these weren't tears of happiness. Uncle Jefferson hung his head as if he were destroyed.

"Jefferson, heavenly days, what is it?" Aunt Gussie said. "I know you've touched him in a deep way, Reverend Faith, but this ceaseless weeping from a man is most disturbing."

Clancy put a big hand out to smother Jefferson's. "What is it, my friend?" he said.

"Can I be excused?' Rudy muttered.

No one answered. Uncle Jefferson lifted his tear-stained face and said, "I have a confession to make. I've done something terrible."

Rudy froze. He wanted to leave the table more than ever now, but he was too stiff with fear to move. This was it. Uncle Jefferson was going to reveal himself as a phony. Rudy had never wanted so much to be wrong.

"Shall we go into the living room?" Clancy said.

"No, I want my whole family to hear this. I've told a terrible lie."

"Oh?" Aunt Gussie said. She sounded a little nervous herself.

"I told you that I had taken care of my acting job so I could stay on here for the rest of the revival."

"But you didn't," Aunt Gussie said.

"Did you get fired, Uncle Jefferson?" Hildy Helen said. "How awful! Those people should be told a thing or two. You're the best actor—"

Uncle Jefferson waved a hand, and they all got quiet. "No, I didn't get fired. I never had a part in the first place."

The table itself seemed to gasp.

"I came up here thinking I could get in with this phony evangelist and maybe travel with him, really jazz up his show. My career in New York is over. I'm too old for the good roles anymore." Uncle Jefferson took a swipe at his dripping nose. "But that very first night, I knew I was a goner. Jesus had me by the throat, and He wasn't letting go. But I've lied to you all, and I'm so sorry. So sorry."

He started crying again, and of course, the women were on him with hugs, and Quintonia brought him a whole new plate of scalloped oysters. Rudy picked up his fork and poked at his, now growing cold in front of him.

What does this mean? he thought. *Does it mean he really is telling the truth? Or is he just playing it bigger and bigger and bigger? He lied to us before. How do we know he isn't lying now?*

Rudy looked carefully at his Aunt Gussie. She looked worried about Uncle Jefferson, the way her face was pinched and her mouth was set. No veins were bulging yet. Rudy just hoped it wasn't a matter of time before they were.

The next day, however, something else happened that pushed that problem to the back of his mind.

The kids were running down the beach chasing seagulls when they heard a zany-sounding horn blowing from the top of the bluff. There was Uncle Jefferson in his gunmetal blue Model A Ford, wearing a white golf cap to shade his tanned face and waving at them.

"I'm taking her for a final spin around the Cape!" he shouted to them. "Come join me, all of you—before I take her out to sell her!"

They bolted for the bluff—all except Rudy.

"Wait!" he shouted. "Where are we all gonna ride? It's a

roadster. There's only one passenger seat."

"Where will we sit?" Hildy shouted up to their uncle.

"On the back, of course!" Uncle Jefferson shouted back. He patted the level just behind him, where the car's trunk was.

"How fun!" Hildy squealed.

She took off again with the rest of them on her heels. But when they finally reached the top of the bluff, Rudy, out of breath and scowling, said, "We can't ride on the back of your car, Uncle Jefferson. It isn't safe."

"Oh, for Pete's sake, Rudy," Hildy Helen said. "Do you have to be such a wet blanket? We're just going around Cape Cod. You can only go so fast, right, Uncle Jefferson?"

"Yeah," Rudy said, "but if Aunt Gussie saw us, she'd likely have another stroke or something."

"Oh, my," Marjorie said. "We couldn't have that."

Rudy turned to stare at her. In fact, they all stared at her, including Uncle Jefferson.

"But, my little roof-sitter," Uncle Jefferson said, "I see you up on the roof over there every night. I thought you had a sense of adventure."

"Oh, I definitely do," Marjorie said. "Definitely. But if Rudy says we shouldn't go, we shouldn't go."

"Ah, caught by the mystique of our Rudolph, eh?" Uncle Jefferson said.

Rudy wished he'd drive the Model A right off the bluff. He cringed as he waited for Marjorie to start babbling on about his "mystique," whatever that was.

"I don't know about that," Marjorie said. "But if he were my brother, I'd listen to everything he said. In fact, I wish Rudy were my brother."

"You can have him," Hildy Helen said, pouting.

But Rudy didn't even wrinkle his nose at her. He was too busy feeling his chest mysteriously puff out.

"So Rudolph has said no. I guess that means I'll have to drive solo," Uncle Jefferson said. "Unless anyone wants to come along on his own."

He looked at them all with arched eyebrows, but nobody was willing to break up the gang, not even Hildy Helen. She did give Rudy one last glare as Uncle Jefferson drove off, but she gave it up as soon as Marjorie said, "I'll race you all back down the bluff!"

Rudy took in another chestful of air. "I don't think that's a good idea," he said. He was certain his voice sounded deeper than usual. "Somebody could get hurt. Besides, I'm thirsty. We need a drink."

Quintonia had made lemonade, and the sweet-tart taste put everyone back in a good mood. It was mid-afternoon hot by then, and away from the cool air down at the water's edge, they all grew lazy. Instead of heading back for the beach, the four of them stretched out on the grass and watched the clouds make pictures in the sky. For once, they played a game Rudy could win.

"I think that one right there," Hildy Helen said, pointing, "is a pair of galoshes, unbuckled of course. That's the modern way to wear them, you know."

"Yeah, we know," Little Al said. "You told us enough times. Only it ain't that at all. That there is a Thompson machine gun if I ever saw one. Ra-da-da-da-da-da-da."

"You're both fulla soup," Rudy said. "That's David with his slingshot, getting ready to let Goliath have it right between the eyes with a stone. And that one over there, that big one, that's Goliath himself."

"Oh," Hildy Helen said. "I see it."

"Yeah! I can even see the stones there on the ground. Good goin', Rudolpho!"

"Who's David and Goliath?" Marjorie said.

Hildy Helen rolled over to her stomach. "You know, like you learn about in Sunday school. Remember, David was the little shepherd boy, and he killed the giant nobody else could take down because he had faith in God?"

Marjorie shook her head.

"You didn't get to that one yet?" Little Al said. "It's my favorite, next to Daniel in the lions' den. Now *there* was a regular guy, that Daniel—"

"No," Marjorie said. "I don't go to Sunday school."

"You got a governess for that, too?" Rudy said.

"No. We just don't go to church."

"But you're still a Christian, aren't you?" Hildy Helen said. She was nodding her head as if to give Marjorie the answer she wanted to hear.

"I don't think so," Marjorie said. "I'm not sure what that is, but I'm pretty sure I'm not one."

"Oh," Hildy Helen said. She looked helplessly at Rudy with a "Well, *say* something!" look on her face.

Oh, now *she wants me to say something!* Rudy thought.

What *did* a guy say to that? He wasn't sure, but it somehow got his chest filling up again. Maybe Marjorie did need a brother, if she didn't even know what being a Christian was.

"I'm tired a talkin'," Little Al said. "Let's go back to the sand dunes."

They went back down to the beach, Marjorie moving very slowly down the bluff and looking now and then at Rudy to make sure he was watching her. He was—just to make sure she didn't do something dumb and get hurt.

Once on the sand, though, she took off and led them to a sand dune they hadn't climbed before.

"Look at this," she said. "I've seen this from the bluff a lot of times, but I was never allowed to come down here when it was sunny to look at it closer."

Rudy's eyes followed to the dune she was pointing to. It was further down the beach than the ones that formed the bowl where Little Al and Rudy had found their chest, and it had a different shape.

"What a weird dune," Hildy Helen said. "It has a dip in the top of it."

Instead of having a rounded or pointed top like the rest of the sand dunes, Marjorie's dune did have a notch in the top, as if some giant seagull had come down and taken a bite out of it. Beyond it was a bunch of scrubby sea vegetation, the kind Rudy hated to walk through. Right at that point was where the beach turned into a sort of desert. They'd never even wanted to walk down that way.

"I've always wanted to climb to the top of it," Marjorie said.

"Then let's go do it," Hildy Helen said. She gave Rudy a long, hard look. "Unless Rudy thinks it isn't safe or something."

Rudy surveyed the dune carefully. "I can't tell much from here," he said in his big brother tone, "but we can go take a closer look. Don't anybody start climbing until I get there."

"All right, *Dad*," Hildy Helen said in a voice like ice.

When they got to the dune, Rudy walked around the front side of it, carefully inspecting how stable the sand was and kicking at a few tufts of beach grass. He wasn't quite sure why he did that, but he could feel Marjorie watching him, and he wanted her to know he was trying to look out for her.

"All right," he said finally. "I guess we can try it."

"There ain't gonna be no tryin' about it, Rudolph," Little Al said. His voice burst out as if he'd been holding his breath. "We're gonna do it!"

He was the first one to reach the top, followed by Marjorie. Hildy Helen only came in third because she stopped to give Rudy a piece of her mind.

"Why are you being so bossy?" she said.

"'Cause nobody else is thinking about our safety," he said.

"Oh, puh-leez. You're just trying to impress Marjorie."

"She wants me to be her brother, so I'm being one," Rudy said. "I thought you were the one who wanted her around."

"I do," Hildy Helen said. Then for some reason Rudy couldn't figure out, she pouted and went on ahead of him.

When Rudy joined the rest, they were all on their knees, feeling the big dip in the top of the dune. Rudy, too, got his hands in it. The sand up there was dug down to the darker, firmer stuff underneath.

"Did the wind do this?" Hildy Helen said.

"Nah," Little Al said. "Or else it woulda done it to the rest of 'em."

He pointed out across the dunes behind them, and the girls looked. Rudy kept studying the worn-down place. There was something familiar about the way it looked, but he couldn't quite put his finger on what it was.

By then it was time to scratch for clams, and then they had a game of tag on the beach. It was actually fun for Rudy—until he had the urge to dump a pail of clams on Little Al's head and had to stop himself. He reined himself in some. He told Marjorie she ought to wear long sleeves the next day so she wouldn't get any more sunburned.

When the sun started to sizzle down into the horizon, Hildy Helen said, "I wish we could stay out longer. I don't want to go to this dumb meeting tonight."

But Rudy did. It was the last meeting, his last chance—maybe to see Uncle Jefferson give up his act, or maybe to have a big experience himself. A new thought even occurred to him.

If it happens to me, he thought, *I'll know it's real for Uncle Jefferson. And then maybe I won't have to always be suspecting that Clancy Faith's a phony, either.*

Rudy just hoped that when Uncle Jefferson finally admitted that he'd been putting on a show, it wouldn't upset Aunt Gussie too much. So far Rudy had been able to keep his promise to Dad and not let her get riled about anything. He wanted to keep it that way.

When they parted with Marjorie at the back gate, she poked with her toe at the mud, worn down by all the feet going in and out, and said, "I'll see you tomorrow."

Her perfectly round green eyes were sad. Even her porcelain hair seemed to droop.

"I wish you could go with us tonight," Hildy Helen said. "It is kind of fun watching all those people dance around. I even do it myself sometimes, and so does Little Al."

"She'd hate it," Rudy said quickly. "She's not a Christian, remember?"

"But I thought that was what it was supposed to be for," Hildy Helen said.

Marjorie's head dropped even further. "That's all right," she said. "I'll just see you tomorrow."

As soon as she was out of sight, Hildy Helen let Rudy have it on the arm with the back of her hand.

"Ouch!" Rudy said. "What was that for?"

"For hurting Marjorie's feelings! Didn't you see the look on her face? You made her feel left out!"

"I just thought—"

"You think too much, Rudy!" Hildy Helen said, and she stomped off toward the house.

"What was that all about?" Rudy said.

"She's just bein' a doll," Little Al said, looking very wise. "What else can I tell ya?"

Rudy had just finished putting on his best summer knickers and a freshly starched white shirt that evening when the front doorbell rang. It was the first time any of them had heard it all summer. They had only had one unexpected visitor, and he had climbed in the back window.

Everybody in the family beat it through the living room, and since Hildy Helen got there first, she threw open the door.

It was the Kelly brothers, holding a trunk between them.

✠ ⬦ ✠

Chapter Fifteen

*B*efore anyone could say a word on either side of the door, Hildy Helen let out a scream that could have ripped a hole in a bed sheet.

Quintonia grabbed her and held her against her chest and glittered her eyes at the two men. Uncle Jefferson put his hands over his ears. Little Al doubled his into fists. Rudy just stood there with his heart slamming.

Only Aunt Gussie remained calm. "What on *earth*, Hildegarde?" she said. "Gentlemen, may we help you?"

"Why don't you just go back inside, Miss Gustavio?" Little Al said as he stepped forward. "We'll take care o' these two thugs, me 'n' Rudolpho."

Rudy finally came to life. He stepped up next to Little Al, barring the way between the Kelly brothers and his family. But his heart was trying to come right out of his chest.

"Oh, for heaven's sake," Aunt Gussie said. "This is not Chicago! These men are quite obviously not thugs. Have all three of you taken leave of your senses, or just your manners?"

"Yes, they are too thugs, Aunt Gussie!" Hildy Helen cried. "We saw them—"

Rudy and Little Al turned on her like a pair of mad dogs after the same bone, both growling at the same time.

"Hildy Helen, take Aunt Gussie to the kitchen and get her calmed down."

"Come on, doll, quit squawkin' and get everybody outta here so we can take care a this."

"Silence!"

And there was, of course, silence, because when Aunt Gussie raised her voice, everybody obeyed. Even Uncle Jefferson, who suddenly looked smaller in his pink and blue suit, kept quiet. Hildy Helen did try to get out one, "But Aunt Gussie," but she shut up fast when she saw her aunt raise her palm to the air. That wasn't what frightened Rudy. It was the veins bulging in Aunt Gussie's neck. His heart speed doubled.

"Now then," Aunt Gussie said, "if I may be allowed to speak for myself instead of being treated like some sort of invalid." She gave the kids one more dagger stare before she turned to the Kelly brothers, who were waiting patiently on the doorstep. "Gentlemen, I do apologize, but the children seem to have mistaken you for Chicago hoodlums. I'm sure you know what a violent city we come from and will judge them accordingly."

The tall blond removed his tan fedora and twinkled his blue eyes at Aunt Gussie. She smiled right back at his freckles.

Maybe Aunt Gussie's not so good at spotting a phony as I thought, Rudy told himself.

Or maybe they're not bad guys after all. We didn't stop to talk to them that night, and it was dark, and—

But his next glance, at the other, broad-shouldered Kelly brother wiped that thought right out of his mind. Curly was looking right at Rudy, with a smirk on his lips. He couldn't have said, "Give it up, kid. You're way out of your league," any more clearly if he'd spoken the words out loud.

Rudy looked at Aunt Gussie. *Look at this guy's face!* he wanted to shout at her.

But she was already intent on the sea chest Blondie was showing her. And so was Little Al. By now, he didn't seem to care *how* upset Aunt Gussie got. He thumped it firmly with his thumb.

"Hey, Rudolpho," he said, "this is our chest!"

"Yes, it is, my boy," Blondie said. "And we're returning it to you, just as we said we would."

"Sorry it took us longer than expected," Curly said, the smirk gone from his lips, "but we were unexpectedly called to Europe, and then when we got back, we had to take it to several different dealers before we found one who could remove the padlock without leaving any markings on the piece itself."

"I see you got it took off, though," Little Al said. "What was in it?"

"Exactly what is in it right now," Blondie said. "I can't wait to see the looks on the faces of you two fellas when you get a look at it. You mind if we set this down, madam?" he said to Aunt Gussie. "It's getting a bit heavy."

"Yeah, set it down and beat it," Little Al said. "The trunk's ours."

"It certainly is yours," Curly said. "We had it examined in Provincetown by an expert, and it seems I was mistaken. It isn't 1790s vintage."

"1910, can you believe that?" Blondie said to Aunt Gussie. "It's not worth the time it took to make it into a replica. I'm sure you share my disgust when someone tries to pull a caper like that, don't you—you having an interest in antiques yourself."

"How did you know I was interested in antiques?" Aunt Gussie said.

"The Cape is a small place. You'd be surprised how quickly the word gets around. Was it Zork, Michael, who told us—"

"Not half as surprised as I'm going to be when I find out how you happen to know my boys and how this sea chest has anything to do with them," Aunt Gussie said.

By that time, Rudy's head was spinning. Little Al looked like he wanted to run the two of them off at gunpoint. Hildy Helen had recovered from hysteria and was curiously fingering the chest. Rudy didn't know *what* to do. The longer Aunt Gussie talked, the bigger her veins got. And what about the Kelly brothers? Were they the hoods or the good guys?

He'd almost decided to just open his mouth and let the first thing that was in there come out and hope it was something responsible, when another voice joined the confusion—a low, reedy clarinet voice.

"Mrs. Nitz, is there a problem I can help you with?"

It was Sandy Potter, saving the day again. Rudy resisted the urge to throw his arms around the man's neck. Besides, Marjorie was with him. Rudy filled his chest and stepped forward.

"Hello, Mr. Sandy," he said. "We were just trying to sort out—"

"Hush, Rudolph," Aunt Gussie said. "Mr. Potter, apparently my boys had some kind of deal with these two gentlemen, which we will 'sort out' later—"

She pointed her pencil-sharp eyes at Rudy. He took a step back again. He hoped Marjorie hadn't noticed that too much.

"They appear to be holding up their end of it," Aunt Gussie said, "and we were just about to examine the contents of this chest. Care to join us?"

"Buried treasure, eh?" Mr. Sandy said, smiling as always. He propped a long, pinstriped leg up on the step and said, "I'd love to. Always wanted to discover some treasure." He nodded politely to the Kelly brothers then, and they nodded back. "Sandy Potter," he said.

"Pleased to meet you," the brothers said.

"It seems as if we should have some sort of drumroll," said Uncle Jefferson from the back. He was filling up his suit again, and the impish glow was back in his eyes. "Shall I?"

"Oh, please, can we forego the dramatics and just get this done?" Aunt Gussie said. "We've a revival meeting to attend."

"We wouldn't want to keep you," Blondie said. And with a flourish, he pulled a key from his pocket, gave it a twist in the keyhole, and opened the lid.

Immediately there was gasping and oohing and aahing. When Rudy saw what the chest contained, he joined in.

It was more money than Rudy had ever seen in his life—even in Aunt Gussie's purse when she took them on an outing. The bottom of the sea chest was filled with bills, piled neatly in stacks and lined up in straight rows like soldiers in a movie.

Little Al let out a whistle that seemed to last five minutes. Hildy Helen started to let out a scream but quickly plastered her hands over her mouth. Uncle Jefferson began to laugh.

"What is so funny?" Aunt Gussie said.

"Well, it's got to be counterfeit," he said. "What fools would return money people didn't even know they had?"

"These fools," Curly said, pointing to himself and his brother. His face was so serious, so smirkless, Rudy wasn't sure he'd really ever seen him look anything but completely sincere. Blondie looked the same—innocent, even somewhat hurt.

"Can you tell counterfeit money, Mr. Potter?" Aunt Gussie said.

"Oh, yes," Mr. Sandy said. "May I?"

"Of course!"

He slipped a careful hand into the chest while Marjorie stood on tiptoe beside him and watched his every move as if he were a magician. Rudy found himself watching him that way, too.

Mr. Sandy pulled out a bill and held it up to the light and even smelled it. He gave Aunt Gussie a grave look, and all three of the children held their breath.

"This is the genuine article, Mrs. Nitz," he said. "I would say there is approximately $10,000 here."

Hildy Helen did squeal that time, and Little Al looked too

shocked to whistle. Rudy could only stare.

"And speaking of the genuine article," Mr. Sandy said, "that would describe you two young men. What are your names?"

"Michael Kelly, sir," said Blondie.

"I'm Shawn Kelly." Curly shook Mr. Sandy's hand and ducked his head modestly.

"Your parents must be very proud to have raised two such fine men," Mr. Sandy said. "Are either of you interested in a job?"

They looked at each other and smiled. "No, sir," Michael said. "We're quite set, thank you. We enjoy buying antiques—"

"That's a waste," Mr. Sandy said, although his voice wasn't unkind. "With your brand of integrity, you would be a credit to any business."

"If you could find a business with any integrity these days," Aunt Gussie said dryly. But she offered her hand to Mr. Sandy. "I'm sure yours is an exception, Mr. Potter," she said. "Thank you for your help. If I can return the favor in any way—"

"Actually, you can," he said. He smiled down at Marjorie, who Rudy had almost forgotten was there. "My wife and I are holding a little party for a few business associates this evening, and Marjorie has said she gets much too lonely sitting it out up in her room. We were wondering if she could stay the evening with you."

"Yes!" Hildy Helen said. She dropped the handful of bills she was holding back into the chest and grabbed Marjorie instead.

"We would be delighted to have her," Aunt Gussie said, "though I don't know if hysteria is in order."

Mr. Sandy laughed. "Young girls," he said. "We can always count on them for merriment, eh? I'm sure you were the same way as a youngster."

"Oh, I beg to differ," Uncle Jefferson piped up. "I was there. She was born with a set of morals that would shame a saint and had the manners to go with them."

"Then there is no place I would rather leave my daughter," Mr.

Sandy said. "Now then, gentlemen, may I see you to your car?"

Good-byes were said all around, and Hildy Helen pulled Marjorie bodily out of the living room and up the stairs. Mr. Potter and the Kelly brothers strolled like three gentlemen down the clam shell drive, and Little Al and Rudy stood staring into the trunk full of money.

"I'm gonna buy me seven pairs of oxford bags," Little Al said. "What are you gonna do, Rudolpho?"

"He's going to do absolutely nothing except keep his hands off that money. And so are you, Alonzo," Aunt Gussie said.

"But the dough's ours!" Little Al said. It was the closest Rudy had ever heard him come to a wail.

"It most certainly is not. This 'dough' belongs to whomever put it there in the first place—or whomever it was taken from to be put there."

"But we found that trunk fair 'n' square—"

"Right where its rightful owner lost it." She closed her eyes as if she were very, very tired. "I wish your father were here," she said.

I don't! Rudy thought. *Or we'd have some tall explaining to do!*

As it was, he didn't know how they were going to explain it all to Aunt Gussie without her getting even more upset. But she didn't seem too interested in hearing about it now. She simply closed the lid to the chest, dusted off her hands, and called out, "Hildegarde! You and your friend come on. We're going to be late!"

Hildy Helen's stunned face appeared in the living room moments later, Marjorie bouncing in beside her. "But I thought I could stay here since I have a guest," Hildy said.

"You thought wrong. Miss Marjorie can come along with us. Have you ever been to a revival, my dear?" she said to Marjorie.

"She's never even been to church!" Rudy said.

Hildy Helen glared at him so hard he could feel her eyeballs boring into his soul. But he didn't want Marjorie going along, and now he knew why.

When I don't feel anything, when I can't get excited enough to dance around for God, she's gonna wonder if I'm a real Christian.

It was odd even to him how he'd only been her "brother" for a day, and yet he didn't want to let her down.

"Then it's high time she went," said Aunt Gussie. And she swept them all out of the house and into the pink Pierce Arrow.

They were late getting to the tent, and by then people were stuffed inside like candies in a bag and leaking out at every opening. It was "hotter than blue blazes" in there, as Quintonia put it, but Rudy thought maybe it was a good thing it was so crowded. Maybe people wouldn't be doing so much dancing, especially Uncle Jefferson.

But dance they did. Clancy Faith gave his most powerful message yet—the Resurrection story. The minute the Reverend Clancy shouted, "Somebody ought to say amen to that!" women were singing hallelujahs and men were pulling off their summer suit jackets and clapping with arms stretched up over their sweat-soaked shirts. People elbowed their way through the crowd to get to the front so Clancy Faith could lay hands on them and pray for them and they could give their hearts to Jesus and be saved.

But no one put more into it than Uncle Jefferson. He outdid himself that night.

It's his last chance to perform here, Rudy thought.

He glanced from his uncle, who was standing up on a wooden folding chair leading the folks in a frenzy of clapping, to Marjorie, who was glancing around her with a strange look on her face.

But it wasn't that strange to Rudy. He knew it was the same look he had on his own face. *What is going on here?* it said. *Is this real?*

Rudy looked back at his Uncle Jefferson. His head was thrown back, and he was singing and weeping and laughing all at the same time as he praised God right up through the ceiling. Rudy's heart sank.

He looks so happy, he thought. *I want it to be real for him. I want it to be real for me, too.*

Rudy couldn't look back at Marjorie now, because he was starting to cry. Rudy Hutchinson, oldest boy in the house, the one left responsible by Dad, was about to start bawling right there in a crowd of strangers—and in front of Marjorie.

But he couldn't help it. Everyone around him was having some kind of wonderful party with God, and Rudy hadn't even been invited. There was no surge of joy in his chest, no urge to reach his hands up and clap. He didn't even want to move his feet.

But he wanted to want to. And because he didn't, the tears were burning in his eyes.

He felt a soft touch on his sweaty arm, and he jumped. It was Marjorie. She curled her fingers around his damp sleeve.

"What's going on, Rudy?" she shouted over the joyous din. "Are all these people crazy?"

"No," Rudy said, "they're Christians."

"Oh," she said. "Then why aren't you doing it?"

I don't know! he wanted to scream at her. And he wanted to run out of the tent and never be responsible for another human being as long as he lived.

"Rudy?" she said. "Are you crying?"

"No!" Rudy said and slapped the tears out of the corners of his eyes. "I'm just getting . . . getting caught up."

It sounded so ridiculous he wanted to laugh. So he did laugh. He threw his head back and laughed and forced his hands to come together.

"Rudy, my boy!" Uncle Jefferson cried from atop his chair. "Look at you!" Then to Rudy's horror he reached down and with a strength Rudy never would have thought his old uncle had, he pulled Rudy up to the chair next to his and grabbed his hand. "Clap with me, Rudy!" he said. "Clap for the Lord! Let those tears flow! Let Him see that you love Him!"

Rudy did. He had no choice. There were people watching him all over the tent, Aunt Gussie and Hildy Helen—and Marjorie, of course. And the Reverend Clancy Faith, who looked up from the person he was praying over and clicked his eyes right into Rudy's.

Rudy twisted his head away and clapped and sang for all he was worth. He was doing it for Marjorie. But he didn't feel a thing.

It'll make Marjorie know I'm a real Christian, he told himself, *and she'll believe me when I tell her stuff. It's my responsibility*.

And then suddenly Rudy felt a firm hand on his pant leg, and he felt himself being pulled down from the chair. There was a sweaty body close to his and a face with perspiration pouring from it right down onto him. Rudy looked up into Clancy Faith's bullet eyes.

"Don't do it, son," Clancy said in a low voice. "If it doesn't come from your heart, it's a mockery."

Then he let Rudy go and disappeared into the crowd.

✢✦✢

Chapter Sixteen

*T*he revival meeting couldn't be over fast enough for Rudy. Even in its frenzy, the celebration going on around him seemed to plod to its end like an elephant dragging its feet. Rudy left Marjorie clapping her hands in confusion beside Hildy Helen and slumped down on the floor behind the tent flap. When the Reverend Clancy Faith finally quieted the crowd enough to offer up his final prayer, Rudy was the first to bolt for the Pierce Arrow.

"Where are you going, Rudy?" Hildy Helen called after him. "Don't you want to say good-bye to Reverend Faith? He's leaving."

Rudy pretended not to hear her as he ran across the street to the car. Reverend Clancy Faith was the last person he wanted to see, because he was the one person who knew that Rudy was the very thing that he accused other people of being—a phony.

I'm worse than the Kelly brothers. And if I'm a fake, then Uncle Jefferson is, too.

How, Rudy wondered as he crawled into the back seat to wait for the rest, how could he ever have thought he could be the responsible one for Dad? Or the protector for Aunt Gussie? Or the big brother for Marjorie? How could he even have thought he was a Christian?

I mocked God, he thought miserably. *I don't think He forgives you for that.*

It seemed to take another hundred years for the rest of the Hutchinsons and Marjorie to tear themselves away from the revival tent, and when they did, they were still wired up like radio sets and continued their singing as they piled into the car.

Rudy avoided Marjorie by sitting up in the front seat with Sol, who was too deaf to notice whether Rudy was singing or not. But when Uncle Jefferson insisted that they all stop for ice cream before they headed back to Wellfleet, Marjorie planted herself right beside Rudy in the ice cream parlor and stuck to him like a postage stamp.

"I'm glad I went, Rudy," she said to him between spoonfuls of lemon ice. "I know you didn't want me to, but that was only because you thought I would be embarrassed by all that carrying on, but I wasn't. My mother would have been. I can't even imagine her being there. But she wasn't with us, now, was she? And she doesn't know everything. Daddy, he knows just about everything, and you know what, Rudy?"

She took a breath, long enough for Rudy to say, "No, what?"

"You are just like my daddy. I think that's why I like you. Of course, you're not as tall as him, but that's not what I'm talking about. I'm talking about—"

Rudy had no idea *what* she was talking about. His mind snagged on the fact that he was nothing at all like the handsome, wise, responsible Sandy Potter who always seemed to be at the right place at the right time, saying and doing the right things.

I guess she didn't hear what Clancy Faith said to me, Rudy thought. *She still thinks I'm some wonderful big brother.*

But I'm not. I'm a phony.

When finally—*finally*—they got back to the summer house, it was apparent that the "business party" was still going full steam next door. There was a jazz band playing in the backyard, and people were everywhere—on the front porch, among the lilacs, in the yard, and obviously in every lit-up room inside. They were like a kaleidoscope in their bright summer silks and flashing jewelry as they danced in and out of the light of the Japanese lanterns hanging in crisscross patterns over the yard.

"No wonder you hate to sit up in your room with all of that going on without you!" Hildy Helen said to Marjorie as Aunt Gussie ushered them all into the house.

But Marjorie shook her head. "I'd rather be with all of you," she said.

Before she could cast some little-sister type smile in his direction, Rudy hightailed it up the stairs.

Marjorie, of course, wasn't far behind him.

"I have an idea!" she said.

"I like a doll with ideas," Little Al said as he and Hildy Helen joined them in the boys' room. "Whatta ya got?"

"Let's *all* climb out on your roof and watch the party together."

"We can pretend we're guests!" Hildy Helen said. She looked longingly out the window. "I wish I had a feather boa, and some long beads."

Little Al rolled his eyes at Rudy. "I'll never understand dames, Rudolpho."

They all crawled out the boys' window and situated themselves on the little roof above the window below. They had a seagull's eye view of all the goings-on—the couples outdoing each other in the Charleston and the Big Apple; the waiters weaving in and out among them with trays piled up with fruit and cold cuts; the musicians puffing out their cheeks on their saxophones and plucking the strings of their bass fiddles, heads wagging in rhythm.

"We should get up and dance, too!" Hildy Helen said. She was so excited it seemed to Rudy she was ending every sentence with an exclamation point.

Marjorie started to stand up, but Rudy said, "Dance? Good grief, there's barely enough room to sit."

"Wet blanket," Hildy Helen said, losing the exclamation point.

"No, Rudy's right," Marjorie said. "Most boys don't care about whether you get hurt or not, that's what my mother says. My daddy doesn't worry about it so much, but she says they don't watch out for you. But Rudy, he's so mature—"

"Oh, brother," Hildy Helen said.

Rudy was saved from a debate about his virtues by a sudden ruckus from next door. The last strains of the song were still in the air, the partiers were still clapping, and someone was yelling from the far corner of the yard.

All of them turned from Rudy and craned their necks to see. A man in a white tuxedo with a red carnation in his lapel was charging through the dancers, knocking people aside with his elbows.

"Hey, Rudolpho," Little Al whispered near Rudy's ear, "we know that guy."

Rudy squinted his eyes behind his glasses and examined the man's shock of surprised-looking blond hair and the proper way he was trying to stagger up to the bandstand. He did look familiar, but Rudy couldn't place him—until the man opened his mouth.

"Play it again, would you?" the man shouted at the band. "Play that one again. Play it!"

The voice came right out of the man's nose like a silver trumpet.

"Rudy!" Hildy Helen said. "Isn't that Louis? The man who was thrown into the pond?"

It was, but Rudy never had a chance to answer her, for Louis suddenly put an elegant hand inside his tuxedo coat and drew out a gun. Dancers gasped and shrieked and ran for cover under hanging tablecloths. Up on the roof the girls screamed and clung to Rudy and Little Al. Rudy could only stare as Louis pointed the revolver and shot the back right off the bass fiddle.

Splinters of shiny wood flew everywhere, and the bass player stared at the gaping hole in his instrument. The Potters' backyard erupted in an explosion of panic. People ran and shrieked, bouncing off each other like mindless pinballs. At first Rudy was stupefied by it all. And then Marjorie stood up on the little roof and screamed, "Daddy!"

Almost before Rudy and Little Al could stop her, she lunged for the edge of the roof, as if she were going to leap right off and into the yard next door. Rudy grabbed at the hem of her frock, and Little Al got her by the arm. She was still flailing and screaming when a commanding voice shouted, "Quiet, everyone, please!"

The crowd fell into a whimpering hush as Sandy Potter raised his arm above them.

"Ladies and gentlemen, please excuse that outburst. No one has been hurt, thank heaven, and the perpetrator is being removed."

Rudy figured out that the "perpetrator" was Louis, who was just then being carried by the elbows off to the side of the yard.

"I don't know what came over me," he was saying in his silver trumpet voice. "But something did."

Sandy Potter smiled at his guests and said in his own rich, reedy voice, "Some people just get carried away, don't they?"

There was relieved laughter, and a bevy of maids in black dresses and white aprons descended on the splinters of bass fiddle and began to sweep them up. The fiddle player sat, white-faced, in a chair and mopped the sweat from his forehead.

"Carried away, I'll say!" Little Al said.

"That man was out of his mind," said Hildy Helen.

The whole thing reminded me of Uncle Jefferson at the revival meetings, Rudy thought.

He was about to slip back into the window and get away from the whole mess when his eye was caught by Marjorie. For perhaps the first time since he'd met her, she was perfectly still and silent. Her eyes were watching something below, following it like a gull after a fish.

Rudy's eyes followed. It was her father, of course. He went over to Louis, said something abrupt to him and then returned to his guests, touching backs and nodding his head and returning everyone to a party mood.

He does *know Louis—and Marjorie knows he does. And she gets mad every time we bring it up.*

The thought shook Rudy back into his responsibility. "I think we ought to go inside, all of us," he said. "Come on, everybody in the window."

"Why?" Hildy Helen said.

Little Al nodded. "Yeah, Rudolpho. It was just startin' to get good."

"It isn't safe out here, that's why," Rudy said.

"It is *too* safe! How *dare* you make a remark like that? It is *always* safe when my daddy is here!"

Rudy felt his mouth drop open, just the way Little Al's and Hildy Helen's were doing. Marjorie stood with her little white fists clenched at her sides, cheeks scarlet-pink beneath sparking eyes. It was the same Marjorie Rudy had been with on the bluff that first night.

"You just take that back, Rudy Hutchinson, you classless little—sea urchin!"

Rudy shook his head woodenly. "I can't take it back. Somebody just shot a gun off over there."

"Nobody got hurt! Nobody ever gets hurt! The guns are just for precaution—"

"Against what?" Little Al muttered. "Dangerous fiddles?"

"I hate *all* of you!" Marjorie burst out. "I'm going home!"

She made another lunge, this time for the window. Hildy Helen fumbled for her hand, crying, "No, Marjorie! Please don't go! Rudy didn't mean that!"

Little Al whistled, long and low. "That's one doll I definitely don't understand," he said.

But Rudy didn't feel like he'd won or proven a thing. Although Hildy Helen tearfully convinced Marjorie to spend the night after all, provided they stayed in Hildy Helen's room away from the boys, Rudy could feel Marjorie's anger from all the way across the hall. It burned like the stomach flu.

That wasn't all, either. Rudy felt even worse than he had when the Reverend Clancy had told him he was "making a mockery." Now not only was Rudy a phony, but Marjorie apparently was, too. After being her big brother all this time, it was a sad thought.

God? Rudy thought as he lay in bed listening to Little Al sleep. *Isn't there anybody who's real?*

The party finally died down next door, but Rudy still couldn't get to sleep. With the Japanese lanterns out, he could see the fuzzy, yellow light from the lighthouse, and he climbed out of bed and went to the window to watch it.

The light reminded him of God, though he wasn't sure why. He watched it make a track on the water. It was like a path you could walk on. *I wish He did live there. It would be so much easier to just go out there on that light road and ask Him: who's real and who's not? Am I ever gonna be real—or will I always be a phony Christian who doesn't feel anything? Those are the things I'd ask Him.*

Rudy thought about going down to the ocean and getting a little closer to the lighthouse, just because it might make him feel better. He might have done it, if he hadn't noticed the Potters' back door opening. Expecting to see more servants coming out to clean up the rest of the party mess, Rudy almost looked away— until he saw two figures cross into the path of the back porch light.

It was the Kelly brothers.

Rudy put his hand over his mouth to keep from gasping out loud as he watched them stride openly across the backyard to the gate, let themselves out, and move on down the driveway toward the street. They walked with their usual wealthy confidence, not glancing back over their shoulders or attempting to stay in the shadows, not even when they reached Sandy Potter's Peerless, opened the doors, and got in.

Mr. Sandy! Rudy wanted to scream. *Those men are stealing your car!*

But he bit his lip and kept watching. *Of course they aren't stealing it, ya dope,* he told himself. *They were probably in there talking to him about a job after all, and he's lending them his car to—*

To drive down to the beach?

Because that was exactly where they appeared to be taking the elegant Peerless. Its tires crunched in the clam shell driveway and then sank into the sand as it headed toward the bluff.

Rudy sat back on his heels, mind whirling. *What do I do? Do I call the police? No, they haven't done anything wrong—yet. Wake up Marjorie?*

No!

God, please tell me what to do, he prayed. He could feel his stomach starting to panic. Something was wrong with the Kelly brothers driving Sandy Potter's car. They had told him right there in the Hutchinsons' doorway that they weren't interested in a job. And if Mr. Sandy had only just met them that evening, why would he let them drive his big, expensive car anyway—especially down to the edge of the bluff, where Rudy had seen them in the storm?

If the Kelly brothers hadn't just brought him and Little Al a trunk full of money—and if Mr. Sandy weren't Marjorie's father—and if Dad hadn't told him to be responsible for everything, Rudy might simply have crawled back into bed and pulled the covers over his head.

But all of those things *had* happened, and he had to find out what was going on. He went to the bed and shook Little Al.

Moments later they were slipping soundlessly out the back screen door, the spyglass in Little Al's hand. Rudy whispered the story to Al as they padded barefoot through the shadows out to the bluff. When they got there, Little Al scratched his head.

"I don't see no car, Rudolpho," he said. "You sure you weren't dreamin'?"

Rudy's heart fell with a thud he could almost hear. He didn't have his glasses on, but he knew Little Al was right. The Peerless had disappeared. Little Al peered through the spyglass, panning the water, the beach, up to the dunes.

"Holy mackerel, Rudolpho!" he said. "Look at that, would ya!"

He handed the sea glass to Rudy, and Rudy trained it where Little Al was pointing, beyond the sand dune with the funny dip. There, out in the desert beach with all its scrub and stickery bushes, were the Kelly brothers. And there was Mr. Sandy's car.

"What are they doin', Rudolpho?" Little Al said.

"They've got the car on the other side of that last sand dune," Rudy said. "And they're walking out past it, where we never go."

"Yeah, and then what?"

"Nothing yet, they're just walking. No, one of them—it's Michael, no, Shawn—"

"Who cares? What are they doin'?"

"Picking up something and heading toward the car with it."

"What is it?"

Rudy started to laugh. He couldn't help himself.

"What *is it*?" Little Al said. "What are you laughin' at?"

"I'm laughing at what it *isn't*!" Rudy said. He took one more gander through the spyglass and handed it to Little Al. He was so relieved, he was sure he was about to melt down into a puddle.

"It's them bodies you saw!" Little Al said, and then he grunted. "Except they ain't bodies, Rudolpho."

"I know. They're figureheads."

"Yeah, with no legs. Dolls with no legs. I don't think I like dolls with no legs that much, y'know. 'Course, I never met one." Little Al suddenly shivered.

"What?" Rudy said.

"I'm starting to rattle off like Marge. Don't let me do that, Rudolpho."

He gave the glass back to Rudy, who continued to watch the Kelly brothers. They brought a few more figureheads out, and then a sea trunk, which as far as he could tell was just like the one they'd returned to Little Al and him that evening. It was strange, but Rudy was still relieved.

"Now I know they *are* phonies."

"They sure put on some show for Miss Gustavio, is what I say. We was lucky to get that trunk back. 'Course, what good does it do us if she won't let us keep the money?"

"Yeah, well, at least Marjorie's father isn't mixed up in something illegal," Rudy said.

"Whattaya mean?"

"They aren't carting dead bodies around!"

"Yeah, but Rudolpho—"

Little Al's voice sounded so serious, Rudy lowered the spyglass to look at him.

"If they ain't doin' nothin' illegal, how come they gotta sneak around in the dead a night like a coupla Al Capone's men? Somethin's fishy about this, is what I say."

"You really think so?" Rudy said. His heart was taking a dive again.

"Only one way to find out. We gotta get closer so we can hear what they're sayin'."

Rudy didn't have a chance to protest that it didn't sound very safe to him. Little Al was already halfway down the bluff. Besides, maybe this *was* the responsible thing to do. They'd do it for Marjorie—even if she *was* mad at him.

So Rudy crept down the bluff after Little Al and followed him behind the dunes. Al stopped him just as they got to the last one and pointed up to it.

"Now I know why it has that dip," he whispered.

Rudy nodded. He realized now where he'd seen a worn-down place like that before: at the back gate where they trampled in the mud all day. That notch had been caused by feet going back and forth from the beach to the desert beyond the last dune.

The boys didn't take that route, of course, but sneaked out into the darkness amid the scrub. Rudy did exactly as Little Al did and flattened himself on the ground. The blackberry bushes stuck him in the chest through his thin pajamas, but he kept quiet, and he watched.

The Kelly brothers were so intent on what they were doing, they looked to neither left nor right as they went from the car to the desert beach and came back with their arms full of more statues and more sea trunks and loaded them into the backseat. Mr. Sandy's Peerless was weighted down in the back until the bumper nearly touched the sand.

"That's about all we're going to get in this load," one of them said.

He didn't bother to whisper, and his voice carried so clearly in the night air it made Rudy jump. He knew he didn't make a sound, but one of the Kellys put his finger to his lips and said "Shhh— listen."

"To what? You're hearing things. Are you getting the jitters, Shawn?"

"Not likely. This job is so easy it's becoming a bore."

"It won't be long now before our life livens up, though, eh?"

"Don't I know it? And after three years slaving for old Snotter Potter, I'm ready! Coming over to the old lady's house to check up on us like that—"

"And counting the money while he was looking at it. I know he was!"

Their voices got muddled for a moment, and Rudy strained to hear. He managed to make out—

"Nosy little brats . . . knew there was going to be trouble . . .

kid getting so cozy with them."

"They never told anybody about us . . . Potter showering them with candy . . ."

The conversation trailed off as they dusted their hands on their trousers and headed for the car. Rudy held his breath. He had pretty much stopped breathing anyway by this time.

One of them—Rudy had lost track of which one was which—paused with his hand on the door handle. "Have you thought about what you're going to do with your half when we get it back?" he said.

Get it back? Rudy thought.

Just then, with a slam of the car doors and a great revving of the motor, they pulled the Peerless away from the sand dune and headed it back toward the houses.

⁘⋅⬧⋅⁘

Chapter Seventeen

udolpho, they're gonna go steal our money!" Little Al cried when they were gone.

"And they're gonna get Aunt Gussie all shook up. She's gonna have another stroke. We gotta stop 'em!"

But Little Al was already well on his way to doing that. He shot off behind the dunes toward the houses with his legs pumping like pistons.

"They'll see us!" Rudy hissed after him.

Little Al flung over his shoulder, "Too dark," and off he went.

The car had to move so slowly through the scrubby bushes that Al was getting ahead of it. Rudy was hard put to keep up with him, and the effort was making his side ache already.

Even if only he *gets there before they do, that'll be enough,* Rudy thought. *Little Al's tough enough to hold 'em off till I call the police—*

But his thoughts—and his plan—were cut off in a horrible flash of silver. The Kelly brothers had turned on the headlights, and there was Little Al, lit up like he was on Uncle Jefferson's stage.

The door on the passenger side flew open, and Curly Kelly was out before Blondie even stopped the car. He tore off after Al, and Rudy watched in horror as the broad-shouldered man snatched his brother up by the back of his pajama top and held him dangling in the air.

"Where's your pal, fella, huh?" Curly said.

Little Al didn't answer, but he didn't have to. Curly flipped his head around and zeroed right in on Rudy.

"Run, Rudolpho!" Little Al shouted.

He might as well have saved his breath. Rudy whirled around and took off, back toward the desert beach, but he'd barely gone three steps before he felt a strong hand grab at the back of his own pajamas and yank him to a stop. Blondie Kelly plastered a hand over his mouth and said, "You can go easy, or you can go hard, but you're going to go, so why fight it, eh?"

There wasn't a trace of the wealthy college kid with the snappy clothes and the breezy manner. Blondie would have fit right in with Al Capone's gang.

Maybe he's already in it, Rudy thought. At least, that was *one* of his thoughts. There were about a thousand of them spinning in his head, making him dizzy with terror. The only thing that kept him from throwing up the minute Blondie tossed him into the backseat was that Little Al was already there, giving Curly a thorough chewing out.

"Look, kid," Blondie said as he slipped behind the wheel, "you can shut up on your own, or we can shut you up. But I guarantee you, you will shut up."

"Then you're gonna hafta—"

"We'll shut up," Rudy said, and he shot Little Al a warning look.

Al, he could tell, didn't like that choice, but he clamped his jaws together and glared at the back of Blondie's head as he bounced the Peerless back to Sandy Potter's driveway.

"Listen to your friend, kid," Curly said to Little Al. "He might not have your panache, but he's got good sense."

"I ain't got no panache," Little Al said. "I don't even know what that is!"

"Sure, you got it," Curly said. "That means you got style, flash, flair. Your pal here, well, he's a little dull, but—"

"Rudolpho ain't dull! He's got more on the ball than you'll ever have, ya two-bit hoodlum!"

Blondie rocked the car to a stop. "Like I said, kid, dummy up."

Little Al did. Rudy could feel tears forming in his eyes. It was an odd thing to add to his dizzying thoughts, but it made him feel less scared to know that Little Al didn't think he was so dull after all.

Fear took over again, though, as Blondie snatched him out of the car and carried him, practically upside down, through the Potters' side gate and across the backyard. It didn't take a genius to figure out he was headed for the pump house, and so was Curly with Little Al under his arm.

Al kicked his legs and had to have Curly's hand plastered over his mouth because he was protesting so loudly, but the Kelly brothers managed to shove them inside the inky blackness of the pump house and slam the door behind them.

"Don't bother yelling, fellas," Blondie said from the outside, "because the only people who can hear you are the Potters, and they won't lift a finger to save either one of you. They want you right where you are."

"Take a nap," Curly said. "We'll be back."

A bolt slid into place—the Potters were big on locks, Rudy remembered—and their footsteps moved away, but then they stopped. There was low talking.

"What are they saying?" Rudy whispered.

"Somethin' about us knowin' where the trunk is. Leave this to me, Rudolpho. You don't know how to lie."

Rudy waited, wishing he could at least touch Little Al so he'd know where he was in this coal-blackness. The footsteps returned to the pump house, and Blondie's voice came through a crack.

"Where is the old lady keeping the sea trunk?" he said.

"What old lady?" Little Al said.

"The crippled one, walks with a cane. Come on, you know what I'm talking about. You can either tell me easy, or you can make me work for it, but either way, you will tell me—"

"You must be talkin' about Miss Gustavio," Little Al said, as if it had just dawned on him. "Sorry, we don't usually call her no old lady. She's a swell old doll. She can ride a bicycle—"

"All right, all right! Where did she put the trunk?"

"We took it to Provincetown tonight," Little Al said. "Dropped it off with an antique fella there."

"Zork!" Rudy whispered.

"Guy name of Zork. See, Miss Gustavio, she ain't nobody's fool. She wasn't gonna take your word for it that the trunk was 1910. She's having it checked out for herself—"

Rudy felt himself nodding. Little Al had been right. He could never have lied as convincingly as this.

"So what did she do with the money?" Blondie said. His voice was growing tight.

"Left it in there, I guess," Little Al said casually. "See, Miss Gustavio, she don't care that much about money. She always tells us it's who we are that's the real stuff, not how much cash we got, if you know what I mean. See, she goes to church, takes us with her, a course, and—"

"All right, spare me the sermon," Blondie said. "You're lying, and we both know it."

"Forget it, we'll find it," they heard Curly say.

"No!" Rudy heard himself cry. "Don't go in there! You'll scare Aunt Gussie!"

"She'll never know we were there, kid, as long as you keep your mouth shut."

And then they padded away across the grass. Rudy plastered his ear to a crack in the wood to listen. He was sure they went up the back steps of the Potters' house and opened the back screen door. The squeak was too close to be the Hutchinsons' door.

"They ain't gone over there yet," Little Al said. "We got time. We gotta attract some attention and get somebody to get us outta here."

"Who?" Rudy said. "They said the Potters are in on this." Rudy stopped, the worst thought yet at the front of his brain. "You don't think Marjorie knows—"

"Then we gotta get somebody from over at our house. And we can't yell or them two college yo-yos will put gags on us or somethin'."

"How come they didn't tie us up?" Rudy said, voice shaking.

"'Cause they didn't have time. They wasn't prepared for us, which means we got surprise on our side."

"Oh," Rudy said.

"Are your eyes gettin' used to this light?" Little Al said.

Rudy blinked. "Yeah, I can see a little. Only I don't have my glasses on."

"Well, feel around. We gotta find somethin' we can stick out through a crack or somethin'. I don't know—"

He continued to mutter while Rudy ran his hand along the wall and collected splinters in his fingers. He was about to give up and go the other way when his palm hit on something. When he touched it more firmly, it moved, and Rudy gave a shout.

"Shhh, will ya, Rudolpho? What was that?"

"Something fell over. It felt like a body or somethin'."

"You and yer bodies. You got a pretty big imagination, is what I say. Where is it?"

"Over here."

By now, Rudy could see the form of Little Al, who knelt at his feet. Rudy squatted, too.

"This is one a them statue things they was puttin' in the car."

"And pulling out of that boat."

"I wish we could see it. Back when I smoked cigarettes, I

always had a book a matches with me."

Rudy felt something zing through his mind. "Marjorie's stash!" he said.

"Huh?"

"Remember, she brought us out here to show us her cigars and matches, only we found that other trunk and we forgot."

"You think they're still out here?"

"We can hunt!"

So both of them crawled around on hands and knees, digging their fingers behind things they couldn't identify. Once Little Al banged his head on the pump, and Rudy was sure something skittered across his hand. But at last, reaching behind a couple of broken bricks in the corner, he located the matches—and several big, fat cigars.

Rudy struck one of the matches against its cover, and the pump house was suddenly flooded with light. It was amazing what one little flame could do.

He held it high over his head while Little Al examined the statue.

"This one's busted up, just like that trunk was," Little Al said. "I guess this is where Mr. Potso keeps the damaged goods."

"Yeah," Rudy said sadly. It was pretty obvious by now that Mr. Sandy was up to no good. Maybe *he* was the biggest phony of all. Rudy sure had liked him.

"Hey, Rudolpho," Little Al said. "Look at this."

"Ow!" Rudy said. The match had burned down to his finger. He tossed it and struck another one. The light revealed a piece of brown paper wrapped around a dark brown cube. The paper was torn at one corner, and a piece of the cube seemed to have chunked off. The broken part looked like dirt.

"What is that stuff?" Rudy said.

Little Al picked up the broken piece and made a face. "It's kinda oily," he said. He took a sniff. "Ugh, some doll's perfume!"

Rudy could smell it now, too, only he'd never noticed any of the women he knew using *that* much scent on themselves.

"Looks like coffee," Little Al was saying, "but it sure don't smell like it. And I ain't gonna taste it, that's for sure."

"What's it doing in there?" Rudy said.

"I don't know, but this whole no-legs statue is full of them packages. Whatever it is, there's a lot of it."

Rudy had an uneasy feeling. "And whatever it is," he said, "I don't think it's good."

"I believe ya, then. You sure know good from bad."

Rudy snorted. "That's not helping us get out of here, is it?"

The match went out again, and Rudy started to slump back down to the dirty floor of the pump house.

"I got it, Rudolpho!" Little Al said suddenly.

"What?"

"You still got them cigars a Marge's?"

"Yeah."

"Then light up, pal. We blow smoke outta these cracks and somebody's sure to see it and come find out what goin' on."

"Who's gonna see smoke at this time of night?"

"I don't know," Little Al said. His voice sounded a little grumpy. "But you got any better ideas?"

Rudy had to admit he didn't. As much as he hated the thought of sticking the big, brown thing into his mouth, he did it and handed another cigar and the matches to Little Al.

"I don't even know how to do this," he said.

"Stick with me, Rudolpho. I used to smoke in the old days, remember?"

That was true, but Little Al had been a Lucky Strike man. It turned out that puffing on a cigarette was a lot different from smoking a cigar.

"I think ya gotta get it wet first with some spit," Little Al said. "And be sure you got the right end."

Rudy felt around until he was sure he had it, and then got the business end good and juicy. It felt disgusting when he put it in his mouth.

"This is awful, Al."

"So's bein' locked up in here."

Little Al struck yet another match and moved it toward the end of Rudy's cigar. The flame bit into it, and Rudy suddenly had a torch coming out of his mouth.

"Ya gotta suck in on it," Little Al said.

Rudy did. The flame went out, and his mouth filled with smoke.

"I betcha these is good cigars, rich as Mr. Potso is," Little Al said.

Rudy pulled the cigar out of his mouth and coughed from his toes. "If these are good, I'd hate to taste a bad one!"

"Yeah, well, we gotta do it, Rudolpho. It's our only chance a gettin' outta here before they go in and start scarin' the daylights outta Miss Gustavio."

Rudy shoved the cigar back into his mouth and smoked for all he was worth, puffing out through the cracks in the pump house. He hadn't taken two drags before he started to feel green.

"Mine's gone out," Little Al said. "How do ya keep these things lit?"

Rudy watched out of the corner of his eye as Little Al struck one more match. He was busily puffing smoke through a crack and hoping he didn't throw up at the same time, when Little Al said, "Hey, Rudolpho, did you see this?"

Rudy looked at the open matchbook cover which Little Al was pushing toward him. In the light of the still-lit match, Rudy could see writing, done in someone's childish hand.

"What's it say?" Little Al said.

"It says, '1 brokin turnk—"

"What's a 'turnk'?"

"1 brokin lady. 2 brokin chestes of droors." Rudy looked up in time for the match to wink out. "Whoever wrote this sure can't spell."

"It wasn't me!"

Rudy took another choking pull on his cigar and said, in a voice he could barely get out, "I bet it was Marjorie. Those were her matches."

"You think she was keepin' track of the damaged stuff for her old man?"

Rudy's heart sank to the very tips of his toes. "Nah. I don't think so," he said.

But down there in his toes, he did think so. It was the saddest thought yet—sad enough to make him want to get out of here more than ever, and cut off the Kelly brothers before they broke into Aunt Gussie's. Before any of this mess got any worse than it was. He pulled in with all the breath he had on the cigar and tried to blow it out against the crack. But all that would come out was a gasping cough.

"You all right, Rudolpho?" Little Al said.

Rudy shook his head, though he knew Al couldn't see him, but his voice wouldn't work. He just kept gasping and coughing and choking until he was sure he was going to die right there in the pump house.

"Rudolpho! Talk to me, somethin'. Are you dyin'?"

All Rudy could do was shake his head. Little Al took to pounding him on the back while Rudy groped for air. His insides were starting to panic.

"Raise yer arms up over yer head!" Little Al cried. He grabbed Rudy by both wrists and yanked his arms upward.

Rudy took another gasping breath, and this time he got air. He crumpled to the floor and breathed like a northbound train.

"Forget the cigar smoke," he said in a barely-there voice. "I don't think it was working anyway."

"Yeah, besides, I dropped mine," Little Al said.

No sooner were the words out of his mouth when Rudy noticed that the smoke was getting brighter.

"Where did you drop it, Al?" he said.

But there was no need to ask. Suddenly, a flame burst from the corner of the pump house. The legless lady was on fire.

"Give me somethin' to put it out with!" Little Al cried.

He was already tearing off his pajama top, but the minute he tried to smother the flames with it, it shriveled into a black mass.

"That *smells*!" Rudy said as he stooped down to gather up some dirt from the floor.

The heavy perfume smell was so think he could practically hold it in his hands. If Rudy had thought he was feeling sick before, he hadn't felt anything yet.

But he pushed down the urge to vomit and hurled two fistfuls of dirt at the fire, which had by now spread to the pump house wall. Panic was turning to terror, and he hardly knew what he was doing as he dug up dirt and threw it at the flames. Nothing was working, and the fire was pushing them back into the corner.

"Start yellin', Rudolpho!" Little Al said.

They tried, but it was almost impossible. Between the cigars and the smoke and the wretched smell that was swirling out of the now charred legless lady, Rudy's throat was dry and swollen, and he could hear that Little Al's was, too. They sounded like frightened, croaking frogs as they pounded on the side of the pump house and screamed, "Help! Fire! Somebody—help!"

Rudy had never realized before that a burning building is loud—much louder than the voices of two young boys, and certainly louder than anything outside.

But somewhere in the midst of their parched screaming and the roar of the flames that thrust their threatening hands at the boys, a voice filtered through.

"Hang on, boys!" it said. "I'm gonna get you out!"

"Uncle Jefferson!" Rudy screamed back. "Help us! Get us out!"

"Don't panic! Get down and cover your heads!"

Rudy obeyed like a robot, and he could feel Little Al doing the same. They hit the ground, and there was a loud crack, and sparks flew like scattering seagulls. Something hot bounced off Rudy's back, but before he could even feel its pain, he was being pulled by his wrists across the dirt. The wall to the pump house was no longer there.

There was only Uncle Jefferson rolling Rudy on the ground and then throwing himself on top of Little Al.

"Somebody get me some water!" Uncle Jefferson cried out. His throat was closing, too; Rudy could hear it. And it sounded weak and quivery, like an old man's.

From out of nowhere, figures finally appeared with buckets and hurled their contents at the pump house inferno. Uncle Jefferson grabbed a bucket, but someone else, a tall person, said, "You sit down. You're hurt. Somebody call a doctor!"

It was Mr. Sandy. Out of the chaos of smoke and fear, Rudy shouted, "Don't listen to him, Uncle Jefferson! He's a crook!"

"The smoke's gotten to him," Mr. Potter said. His voice was full of concern—phony concern.

"I know what I'm saying!" Rudy shouted.

"Don't let 'em get away!" Little Al cried.

Then still another voice piped up. "They already did, Mr. Sandy." It was Hildy Helen, her words filled with tears and fear. "Marjorie and I just saw them. It was those Kelly brothers. They've stolen your car!"

"Take my Ford and go after them, Potter!" Uncle Jefferson said. His voice was barely more than a whisper by this time, and his face was the color of the ashes blowing from the pump house.

"Let them go," said Mr. Sandy as he knelt beside Uncle Jefferson. "We've got to get you to a doctor, man. I think you've nearly killed yourself saving these boys."

Uncle Jefferson finally caved in and fell back onto the ground. "Are the boys all right?" he said, eyes closed.

"We're fine," Rudy said. "And you're gonna be, too!"

"Just as long as you are, that's all. Thank the Lord."

And then he closed his eyes.

"Uncle Jefferson!" somebody screamed. "Uncle Jefferson, I know you're not a phony! Do you hear me? I know you're not!"

Rudy felt himself being picked up by Mr. Sandy before he realized the somebody was himself.

✢ ✢ ✢

Chapter Eighteen

*R*udy tried to wrench himself away from Mr. Sandy, but the man was too strong, and for a panicky moment Rudy thought he was going to try to lock him up again.

But suddenly Aunt Gussie was there, and Quintonia and Mr. Sandy let him go to them. There were sirens screaming and people barking instructions and Marjorie calling "Rudy! Rudy!" as her mother dragged her into her own house. All Rudy could do through it all was cry, just sob into Hildy Helen's lap.

"I'm the phony," he kept telling her. "Not Uncle Jefferson. I'm the phony."

At first she tried to reason with him. "You are not, either, Rudy," she said. "You're the most honest person in the world. You never do anything wrong anymore."

But Rudy kept shaking his head. "I'm not responsible. Dad's gonna be so disappointed in me. I let Uncle Jefferson die."

Hildy Helen gave up and started to cry with him.

The attendants took the unconscious Uncle Jefferson away in an ambulance, and Aunt Gussie followed in the Pierce Arrow with Sol. Quintonia stayed up with the children all night, and Little Al and Hildy Helen finally went to sleep. Even Quintonia's head nodded, but Rudy couldn't doze off. He felt too miserable.

He was still awake when the back screen door squeaked open and the Reverend Clancy Faith came in. He took one look at the sleeping trio and put his finger to his lips. He motioned with his head for Rudy to join him outside.

Rudy followed with his feet dragging. He knew he deserved the tongue-lashing he was about to get, but he also knew he didn't really need it. He had been punishing *himself* all night long.

When he sank down into the red rocker facing Reverend Faith, however, the preacher's face didn't twist into a scolding scowl. Instead, he reached across for one of Rudy's hands and looked at it.

"It appears you've had quite a night," he said. "Dirt under your fingernails. Soot on your hands. Old wet sand up to your elbows. And you smell like you just escaped from a perfume factory. Do you want to tell me about it?"

"Do I have to?" Rudy said. "No offense, but I feel bad enough already."

"You certainly do not have to," Clancy said. "But I guarantee it will make you feel better. How can you feel any worse, right?"

Rudy wanted to tell him. He wanted to feel better, and the Reverend Faith's smile was so kind.

Still, he'd seen kind smiles before—and he'd been fooled.

"How do I know you're not a phony?" Rudy burst out, and then he buried his face in his dirty hands.

Reverend Clancy didn't answer for a while, and Rudy knew he'd made him angry. Now Aunt Gussie was going to be disappointed in him, too.

But finally a hand came up under Rudy's chin and lifted it, and he found himself looking into a pair of clear bullet-eyes.

"Do you still think your Uncle Jefferson is a—what do you call it?—a 'phony'?"

"No," Rudy said.

"And why not?"

"Because he risked his life saving us last night. He didn't even care about his silk pajamas or anything. He could die, and all because he wanted us to be all right."

"Well, let me reassure you about one thing. Your Uncle Jefferson isn't going to die. I've just come from the hospital. He's doing nicely and is insisting that he be allowed to come back here—although they aren't going to let him for several days, of course, not until those burns on his face start to heal."

"On his face!" Rudy cried. "But he's an actor! He can't have scars on his face!"

"He and I have agreed that we're going to let God take care of that."

"I feel awful," Rudy said. His voice clogged up with tears. "It's all my fault he got hurt."

"Is it?" Clancy Faith said. "You haven't told me what you were doing in the pump house."

"It doesn't matter," Rudy said. "We can't prove anything."

"You don't have to prove anything. Suppose you just tell me. I'm pretty good at detecting the truth."

Rudy sighed and shook his head, but he did tell him. And the more he talked—about everything from the first day they found Louis in the pond in a bag to the moment Hildy Helen saw the Kelly brothers run off with Mr. Sandy's car—the more he wanted to talk. So much had built up inside him over the past few weeks, he didn't realize how full he was. When he was finished, he felt emptied-out and weak.

Clancy Faith patted his knee and said, "I'm going to get you something to eat, son."

"No," Rudy said, "please! Tell me God's gonna forgive me for all this stuff. He is, isn't He? Or have I been too bad?"

A gentle smile flickered across Clancy's face. "You're asking me? But I thought I was a phony!"

"No, you're not," Rudy said. He shook his head, which was feeling much clearer now. "Uncle Jefferson told Mr. Sandy to take his car and chase after those thieves. Anybody that can get Uncle Jefferson not to care about his car anymore can't be a phony."

The flicker turned into a broad smile, and Clancy Faith gave Rudy's shoulder a squeeze. "You're a good man, Rudolph Hutchinson, just like your aunt says you are."

But Rudy shook his head again. "I'm not much of a man," he said. "My dad left me to be responsible, and look what I've done."

"I can only think of one thing you've done wrong."

"You'll think of more if you put your mind to it," Rudy said.

Clancy chuckled. "No, I think there is only one. You took what your father said too much to heart. I'm sure he didn't mean for you to carry all of this by yourself. The very first time something went wrong—when you discovered that Louis fellow drowning in a bag—you should have told your Aunt Gussie right away. Maybe all of this could have been avoided."

"But Dad said she wasn't to be upset!"

Clancy gave a soft snicker. "I think it would take a lot more than that to get that strong woman upset. Now last night, she was upset. She thought she was going to lose the two of you *and* her brother."

"She didn't have another stroke, did she?"

"Is that what you're so afraid of?"

Rudy nodded. The tears were starting to come again. He seemed to have no control over the blasted things right now.

"Then I say we put that into God's hands. You can't protect your Aunt Gussie from life itself, and unfortunately in these times, that kind of thing *is* life. She brought you children here to escape the violence and crime in Chicago, and it seems it's found you here, too."

Rudy smacked at the tears. "I'm pretty sure Mr. Potter is a crook, only he's not like the ones in Chicago."

"I don't know much about that," Clancy said. "But I think your father will be able to explain all that."

"He knows?"

"Your Aunt Gussie called him last night. He's on his way to the Cape right now."

"Uh-oh," Rudy said.

Clancy's eyebrows went up. "What 'uh-oh'? Rudolph, you have handled everything wonderfully well, except that you never turned to a grown-up who could help you."

"I kept thinking I couldn't trust anybody else and that I had to be so responsible."

"Did you ever think of asking Jesus for help?"

"Yeah," Rudy said. "But I'm having trouble drawing."

"You're going to have to help me out with that one."

Rudy explained how he always drew his prayers and that now all his drawings seemed the same, flat and dull. "Like me," he said.

"We'll get back to that comment later," Clancy said. "I like this drawing approach. Very good. And I think I know why your drawings have lost life."

"Why?"

"Because it's time for a fresh look at your subject."

"My subject?"

"Jesus. What have you learned from the revival meetings?"

"That I'm not a real Christian."

Reverend Clancy's mouth fell open. "What?"

"I'm not a true Christian like the others. I don't get all emotional about it. You even said I wasn't feeling it."

"I said you weren't feeling the dancing and the shouting. I think you feel very deeply, Rudy. Tell me what you've learned."

"About Jesus—from you?"

"Yes."

Rudy didn't even have to think about it that long, even as exhausted as he was. "He likes people that help other people, even when it's not easy. He likes you to give all you have, even if it's not that much—"

Clancy Faith was shaking his head, and Rudy stopped. "No?" he said.

"Oh, exactly the opposite. You think you're not a real Christian? I would put you up against anybody who danced in that tent! Not only have you learned what I've been talking about, Rudy, but from what you've told me, you're living it."

"I am?"

"You've been a Good Samaritan to Marjorie. You've given all you had for Aunt Gussie, even at the risk of having the other children mad at you. I could go on and on—and you know I can do it!—but Rudy, my point is, you don't have to jump up and down to show that you love Jesus. Jesus wants you to be *exactly* who you are! And you know what happens when people become something they aren't."

"They get to be phonies."

"Like your neighbor, Mr. Potter, whom we have yet to sort out."

"And those Kelly brothers. They work for Mr. Potter. They're disgusting. And Marjorie."

"How is she a phony?"

"She showed me who she was when I first met her, and then she started putting on this big act so she could protect her father from us finding out about him."

"Hmm. That's interesting. I think whether you're right remains to be seen. Now, about your attitude about Jesus. You said a while ago that you thought you were dull. Where on earth did you get an idea like that? Certainly not from our Lord."

"No."

"Good, because He doesn't make dull people. People only become dull themselves when they try to be something they aren't."

"I was trying to be responsible." Rudy's heart dove. "Does that mean I'll never be the responsible person my dad wants me to be?"

"No, it means you don't have to stop being a kid to do what's right and to handle the things a kid can handle. You were trying to control your aunt's health, keep three other children on the straight and narrow, solve a crime, discern phonies from the real thing—" Clancy took a big breath. "I'm exhausted just thinking about all of that! I don't even know an *adult* who could do it."

"But Dad said—"

"When your dad gets here, you talk to him about what he meant. I think you'll be surprised."

Rudy nodded. His head was starting to spin again, and it was as if Clancy Faith could see it. He put out his hands and engulfed one of Rudy's in them. "I'm going to pray, Rudolph," he said. "And then we're going to have a bite to eat, and then you're going to soak in a bath. Then I suggest you go through the day just being responsible for Rudy. Everything else is taken care of. When it's time for you to draw a prayer again, you'll know it. Agreed?"

"I guess so," Rudy said. But the minute the Reverend Clancy Faith started to pray, the tears fell. And Rudy knew he was right.

He was also right about Dad coming. He and LaDonna showed up at noon, with Aunt Gussie, whom they'd picked up at the hospital. They had good news about Uncle Jefferson: He was resting comfortably and said to keep digging those clams because he was going to be home soon and he wanted plenty of chowder waiting for him.

"Giving me orders all the way from the hospital bed," Quintonia said. She smiled in a way Rudy had almost never seen her do before. "He'll be all right," she said.

In spite of what Reverend Faith had said, Rudy only hugged Dad once and then made it a point not to be alone with him. But when they were all gathered around the table for oyster stew and cranberry muffins, Dad looked right at him and said, "Uncle Jefferson did say something that puzzled me. He said to ask you about it, Rudy."

Rudy swallowed an oyster piece whole.

"He said that when the pump house was burning down, he smelled something he had smelled many times before among his actor friends. It was opium."

"Opium!" Little Al said, spoon clattering to the table. "I heard a that. That's bad stuff. It's bad for you. It makes you do loony stuff!"

When he realized the entire table was staring at him, Little Al added quickly, "I never smoked none of it myself. I just heard about it when I was helping the Mob—back in the old days."

"I understand," Dad said.

"The Mob didn't never handle that stuff—only booze. That's bad enough, a course, but opium—"

"It's terrible," Aunt Gussie said. "It can ruin a person's life, even kill him."

"That's right," Dad said. "And Uncle Jefferson said he was certain that was what he smelled in the pump house."

"Is it brown like dirt, only kind of oily?" Rudy said. "Comes in blocks?"

"Yes."

"That was what was stashed inside the figurehead, then," he said.

"Are you sure it was a figurehead, Rudolph?" Aunt Gussie said. Her spoon was suspended midway between her bowl and her mouth.

Rudy shrugged. "I don't know. I've never seen one. We couldn't find one in any of the antique shops, remember?"

"I do, and I found it strange," Aunt Gussie said.

"It ain't strange no more," Little Al said. "Them Kelly brothers has 'em all. They was smugglin' 'em in on boats and hidin' 'em in the dunes and then cartin' 'em off in Mr. Sandy's car."

"And probably using the antique dealers as their cover," Aunt Gussie said, "which was probably why that Mr. Zork became so agitated when Potter came into his shop."

"Nuh-uh!" Hildy Helen said. Her eyes were already shooting sparks. "Marjorie's father would never do anything that was against the law!"

"We'll get to that later," Dad said. "But for now, let's put this together." He stirred his soup, but so far he hadn't taken even a sip. "You found a figurehead in the pump house—which so far I

have no idea why you were locked in at that hour of the night—
we'll get to that later, too—and inside—"

"The statue was broke open," Little Al said.

"I see. And inside was—"

"*Were,*" Rudy said, "a whole slew of brown bundles with that
brown stuff—that opium, I guess—in them."

"Good heavenly days," Aunt Gussie said. Her voice was dead
somber. "They were using antiques to smuggle dope?"

"The Mob doesn't never smuggle no dope!" Little Al said.

"No, they don't usually," Dad said. "They do enough miserable
things without adding that to it. But we aren't talking about the
Mob here."

"No, we're not," Hildy Helen said. Then she gave her head a
nod as if that were the end of the conversation.

But it wasn't. "If what Uncle Jefferson said is true, we may have
something serious to deal with," Dad said.

"But didn't the statue burn up with the pump house?"
LaDonna said.

It was the first time she'd spoken, and Rudy barely recognized
her voice. She sounded so grown-up.

"That's true," Dad said. "Although from what I know, opium
would take forever to burn away. Perhaps there is still some out
there."

He even started to get up, but Clancy Faith put up his hand.
"There is *nothing* out there. By the time I got here at dawn, the
entire backyard had been leveled. Quick clean-up job."

Dad sank back into his chair.

"Then we have no physical evidence," LaDonna said. "Only
Uncle Jefferson's statement."

"Mercy!" Quintonia said. "You are sounding like a lawyer yourself, girl!"

"She'd make a fine one," Dad said. "I don't know what I would
have done without her this summer."

"Back to the case," LaDonna said briskly. She folded her hands, with their pink-painted nails, on the table. "Can you really take this to the police without any physical evidence? Uncle Jefferson and Rudy and Al would make good witnesses, but without tangible proof—"

"The police?" Hildy Helen said. She was near tears. "You're going to turn Marjorie's father in to the police?"

"I might have to, Hildy," Dad started to say.

But Hildy Helen broke right in. "Then I won't be speaking to you for a while!" she said. She scraped her chair back from the table. "Marjorie is the first girlfriend I've had a long time, and now you're going to make her hate me! Rudy already tried, and now you're going to finish the job! I just hate—everyone!"

With that she stormed out of the room and clomped up the stairs.

Rudy felt like a part of himself had just been torn off and dragged with her. "You want me to go talk to her?" he said.

But Dad just took off his glasses and rubbed the bridge of his nose. "No, let her go. This is upsetting, and I don't think anything any of us could say to her right now would make a difference until she calms down."

"Reverend Faith could calm her down," Rudy said.

Aunt Gussie's silver eyebrows shot up. "I see we've had a change of heart in the last 24 hours!"

"Just a little understanding is all," Clancy said.

"You are truly a miracle worker, Reverend Faith," Aunt Gussie said. "The effect you have had on the entire Cape will be felt for a long, long time."

"For eternity, I hope," Clancy said. "But that's just God."

"Still, I don't think the love offering you received for your work nearly comes close to what you deserve—and what you'll need if you're going to continue on."

"Love offering?" Dad said.

Aunt Gussie explained about the collection they took up every night. Rudy didn't listen. His mind was spinning off in another direction. When she was finished, Rudy cleared his throat and looked at his aunt. "If nobody claims that money in the trunk, could I give my half to Reverend Clancy?"

"What money? What trunk?" Dad said.

"We've missed a lot," LaDonna said dryly.

"Take notes, would you?" Dad said to her.

"We'll explain later," Aunt Gussie said. "Rudy, that is a marvelous idea. I am as proud of you as I can be."

And then she did something Aunt Gussie *never* did. She beamed. For a minute there, she looked just like Hildy Helen—young and excited and glowing. Certainly not like a lady who was about to have a stroke any time soon.

"I forgot all about the trunk!" Little Al said. "'Course I gotta be honest. I'd like to have at least one pair a oxford bags outta that dough, but you're pretty swell, Reverend Faithful, and if Rudolpho trusts ya, then I do, too. You can have my half."

The Reverend Faith cleared his throat, too, but Rudy could tell it was because he was getting choked up.

"I am deeply touched," Clancy said. "And I would be the last one to throw a fly into the ointment, but, Rudy, are you certain the Kelly brothers didn't get in last night and take it?"

"They couldn'ta done that!" Little Al said. "Not with all that was goin' on."

"I didn't hear anyone trying to get in, even before the fire," Aunt Gussie said.

"You'da heard that, I betcha." Little Al's voice was spiraling up hopefully. "Nobody came in here shootin' off tommy guns and—"

"But remember," Dad said, "we're not dealing with the Mob. I'm thinking this is an equally dangerous type of criminal—someone with political connections and a lot of money behind him. Someone with smooth manners and good breeding."

"Good breeding?" Clancy Faith said. "Rudy told me about finding one of their men in a bag left to drown!"

Dad shook his head sadly. "That was obviously some enemy of Mr. Potter's, seeking revenge—and probably just as well-bred as he is. You can't be in crime for too long without having to resort to violence. I suppose they all turn out like the Mob in the end."

By now, Rudy was about to explode, and Little Al with him.

"Can we go look in the trunk?" Rudy said.

At a nod from Dad, they were off. Rudy came back five seconds later and said sheepishly, "Uh, where is it?"

"In the living room, right by the door where they left it," Aunt Gussie said.

No one waited for the boys to report back. The entire family went with them, and Clancy Faith, too. There was one big sigh of disappointment when Rudy turned the key and Little Al lifted the lid. The 1910 sea trunk was empty.

"Reverend Faith, I am so sorry," Aunt Gussie said. "I had my hopes up."

"Who knows, Mrs. Nitz?" he said. "Certainly if it was stolen money or opium money, I wouldn't want it anyway."

But Dad's mind was elsewhere. He was getting that faraway look in his eyes, the one he got when he was really digging into a case. Rudy was glad Hildy Helen wasn't there to see it. He kind of wished he weren't, either.

Because no matter how miffed he was that the Kelly brothers had stolen the money—and even how disappointed he was that Mr. Sandy might be selling that opium stuff to people to ruin their lives with—the worst part now was Marjorie. The more they found out, the less likely it seemed that she could have lived in that house over there and not known that something shady was going on.

I didn't want her to be a phony! Rudy thought miserably. *I wanted her to be who she was when she was with us.*

I wanted to be her big brother.

Rudy looked at his father, who was standing and looking into

the empty trunk, arms folded, face squinted into its thinking position. At least he was here to make everything all right again.

And then, suddenly, it hit Rudy. It didn't matter what Marjorie
knew. She had just been protecting her father—and she loved him
just the way Rudy loved his own dad. If Mr. Sandy was taken off to
jail, Marjorie might go right back to being that strange, awful creature she was the night Rudy had first met her.

That was it, of course. When you weren't being who you really
were, you were awful. She couldn't be who she was when she was
so unhappy without her father.

Rudy put his hand on the lid of the trunk. "Well, I guess that's
it. No evidence, no proof. Too bad. You want me to close this up
and put it on the trash, Aunt Gussie?"

"Wait a minute, Rudy," Dad said. "Auntie, what did you say ear-
lier about them smuggling the opium in the antiques?"

"Just that. They put that horrible substance inside the figureheads and the trunks—"

"And that's why they didn't want us havin' it that day on the beach
when we found it," Little Al said. "It was stuffed with packs a opium
right there, Rudolpho! We was about to catch 'em red-handed!"

"I'm beginning to see," Reverend Clancy said. "From what
Rudy told me, these Kelly brothers took the trunk away for a while
and then brought it back full of money."

"They thought you would be so delighted with all this new-
found wealth you wouldn't think anything else about it," Aunt
Gussie said. "That's our present society for you. Nothing but
money, money, money—"

But Dad paid no attention to any of them. He got down on his
knees and ran his hand around inside the trunk. The finger he
brought up was covered in oily brown.

"You did it again, Mr. James," LaDonna said. She produced her
pen. "What shall I write down?"

Dad sniffed his finger. "I'm not certain. We'll have to have it tested, but I think we might have our evidence."

Things moved much too fast for Rudy after that. The police came and took the trunk away. Just an hour later the phone rang, and Dad's face grew somber as he listened. When he hung up, he said, "It was opium. Apparently the smarter bootleggers who run alcohol know that Prohibition isn't long for this world, and they're looking for other ways to make money. Mr. Potter is obviously one of them. They'll be along to arrest him shortly."

Rudy tore up the stairs to Hildy Helen's room and didn't even knock before he plowed in. She was on her stomach on her bed, looking red-eyed and angry.

"Go away," she said.

"They're coming for Mr. Sandy."

Hildy Helen picked up her pillow and threw it at Rudy. He ducked and then grabbed her wrists before she could find another weapon.

"Let go of me, Rudy!"

"I will," Rudy said again. "But you gotta promise that instead of beating me up, you'll go over and talk to Marjorie. You gotta tell her before the cops come."

Hildy Helen stopped struggling and looked at him. "Oh, yeah, that's right, isn't it?"

"She'd do the same for you, I know she would."

Hildy Helen nodded as she slid off the bed and looked around for the shoes she had evidently thrown on her arrival. "She only gets crazy when she's scared, Rudy."

"Yeah, I figured that out."

"She was never scared with us."

Rudy just shook his head and followed her downstairs.

But when they got to the kitchen, it was empty, and the back door was still squeaking closed.

"Where did everybody go?" Rudy said.

Hildy Helen ran to the window. "The police are already here!"

she cried.

She raced out the back door, Rudy right behind her. Outside, in the front yard next door, they found their family and the Reverend Clancy Faith standing in a knot as four policemen emerged from their boxy squad cars.

The front door opened, and Mrs. Potter with her porcelain-perfect hair stepped out, framed by innocent bridal wreath flowers. She closed the door behind her, but it opened again with a jerk, and Marjorie stormed out onto the porch. It was clear she wasn't going to be left out this time.

"Is Mr. Potter at home?" said one of the policemen in his clipped New England accent.

"No, he is not," Mrs. Potter said. The silver-flute voice came out of her nose. "Is there a problem of some kind?"

"There might be," said the policeman. "According to Mr. Hutchinson here—" he waved an arm toward Dad—"Mr. Potter is under suspicion for a rather serious crime. Please tell us where he is, madam, or we'll have to procure a search warrant."

But Mrs. Potter was no longer looking at the policemen. Slowly she turned her face toward Dad, and then she bore down on him from the porch like an angry goose.

"You?" she said. "You sent these policemen here?"

"It had to be done, Mrs. Potter," Dad said. He wasn't using his lawyer voice. *He sounded kind—really kind*, Rudy thought. *Not like the phony Mr. Sandy.* "I'm so very sorry, but it was the right thing to do."

"So much for Christian charity," Mrs. Potter said. "A decent Christian man would never point his finger at a neighbor. Is it any wonder I refuse to go to church?"

"Stop it, Mother!"

The voice that broke into Mrs. Potter's tirade was loud and it was shrill and it was very upset—but it wasn't crazy. Marjorie stepped between her mother and Rudy's father and stabbed her hands onto her hips, Hildy Helen style.

"Rudy *is* a Christian!" she said. "And if he says it's the right thing to do, then it's the right thing to do!" She fixed her very round green eyes on Rudy. "Is it, Rudy? Do you think so?"

Rudy looked at his father, and he knew his eyes were begging. But Dad only nodded toward Marjorie. His eyes said, *You can do it, Rudy. You're responsible enough.*

Rudy took a breath, but his chest didn't puff out. He wound up saying the whole thing to the toe he was digging into the velvet lawn.

"I know how much you love your dad," he said. "Just like I love mine. But what he's doing is wrong, and it's ruining people's lives. Maybe they can help him while he's in jail or somethin'."

"That is quite enough!" Mrs. Potter said. Her face was white and stricken with horror.

But Marjorie was nodding until her china-doll bob swayed. Tears streamed down her pink cheeks like wet stripes, but she said, "I knew he was doing something bad. I even started keeping a list. I couldn't tell on him. But Rudy says we should." She took a tearful breath. "It's the right thing to do."

Rudy never saw Marjorie after that. She and her mother left that very afternoon, and later the police came and searched the house and locked it up and put big signs on it, threatening anyone who tried to enter.

"There will be an investigation," Dad told the children as they sat forlornly on the back porch. "So far they haven't located Mr. Potter—but they will. A man can't run all his life."

Aunt Gussie encouraged them over the next few days to look at all the good things that were happening. Uncle Jefferson was coming home from the hospital. Reverend Clancy Faith was going to stay with them for a week so he could pray with Uncle Jefferson while he regained his strength and faced the surgeries that would fix his face. Dad and LaDonna were staying for a while, too, and when she wasn't taking dictation, LaDonna would be free to explore the beach with them.

But none of that filled the huge notch that had been carved out of their summer life—Hildy Helen's, Little Al's, and especially Rudy's. It reminded him of the dip in the top of the sand dune, worn down by the Kelly brothers' feet.

But at least the empty feeling did one thing. It got Rudy to take out his sketch pad and his pencils and sit on the bluff to draw and listen to the friendly rhythm of the ocean. He drew and he prayed and he drew some more. When he was finally finished, he saw a shadow go over the paper, and he looked up to see Reverend Faith standing there.

"I felt myself being pulled right out here to see your artwork, Rudolph," he said. "I hope you don't mind."

Rudy shook his head. "Want to see?"

Clancy took the sketch pad and squatted down to study it. Unlike a lot of people, he didn't just say, "Swell, son. You sure can draw." Instead, he looked at it for a long time. And when he was finished, he said, "This is for Marjorie, isn't it?"

Rudy nodded. "It's my new look at Jesus. The lighthouse represents Him and the path of light is the Way—how we get to Him. Kind of like a prayer."

Clancy Faith cocked his head. "The only thing I don't understand is the seagull. What does he have in his mouth?"

Rudy shrugged, but he also grinned. "That's a cigar. 'Cause you have to remember that if you try to act too grown-up, God'll be there to remind you who you really are."

He waited for the laugh. For the ruffling of his hair by an adult hand.

But all the Reverend Clancy Faith said was, "Somebody oughta say 'Amen.'"

"Amen," Rudy said. And he meant it.

✟·✟·✟